Surviving Planet Zorone

by

Jane Greenhill

Surviving Planet Zorone

COPYRIGHT © 2021 by Jane Greenhill

Cover Art by *Jennifer Greeff*

The Wild Rose Press, Inc.
PO Box 708
Adams Basin, NY 14410-0708
Visit us at www.thewildrosepress.com

Publishing History
First Edition, 2021
Print Trade Paperback ISBN 978-1-5092-3674-9
Digital ISBN 978-1-5092-3673-2
Previously Published as Comic Books from the Evil Plant Xoron and Evil Comic Books from Planet Zorone

Published in the United States of America

"I've got to tell you I'm counting the days until that bloody moon burns itself out. Now, before I was interrupted by that darnite light, I was about to tell you something exciting. You're the chosen one," Brabora said.

"Chosen for what?" Esoong asked, shading his eye again for the moon's second rotation. Nothing much got done during the day until the fifth star passed through their solar system, and then darkness came.

"The elders are relying on you. You proved yourself with the invasion of Mars and by sending that spaceship to Area 51 on Earth, which threw those Idiotic Earthlings off our scent. It was good work. Exceptionally good work."

"Thank you. Even all these years later, they don't have a clue," Esoong boasted.

"Yes, that's true," Brabora nodded. "Anyway, when the fourth sun passes by, you'll be hologrammed onto Earth. Your mission is to take command of their resources. Then we'll be in a prime position to hold Planet Earth hostage."

Dedication

To Geoff, Adam and Liam who make me more proud
each and every day.

Prologue

"Your patience has paid off," Brabora said to his underling Esoong.

Sighing deeply, they both dropped from the upright position to their four legs and used their extended tails to cover their central lobes.

A species of highly evolved Komodo dragon, they were left extremely sensitive to the light from the turquoise moon circling their planet Zorone.

As the moon rotated away, Esoong gazed in adoration at the senior Zoroneite. He scratched his reptilian forehead with his left claw. Scales broke off in the dry heat, disappearing as they hit the clay base of the planet.

"I've got to tell you I'm counting the days until that bloody moon burns itself out. Now, before I was interrupted by that darnite light, I was about to tell you something exciting. You're the chosen one," Brabora said.

"Chosen for what?" Esoong asked, shading his eye again for the moon's second rotation. Nothing much got done during the day until the fifth star passed through their solar system, and then darkness came.

"The elders are relying on you. You proved yourself with the invasion of Mars and by sending that spaceship to Area 51 on Earth, which threw those Idiotic Earthlings off our scent. It was good work.

1

Exceptionally good work."

"Thank you. Even all these years later, they don't have a clue," Esoong boasted.

"Yes, that's true," Brabora nodded. "Anyway, when the fourth sun passes by, you'll be hologrammed onto Earth. Your mission is to take command of their resources. Then we'll be in a prime position to hold Planet Earth hostage."

Chapter 1

"Greggy, if I've asked you once, I've asked you a hundred million times, clean up your room. If you don't get it done today, I'll do it for you, and you know what that means."

I pulled the duvet over my head in the hopes of drowning out my mom's shrill voice, but it seemed to echo even under the covering.

"Mom, it's the weekend, give me a freak'n break. I'll do it tomorrow." I stifled a yawn and attempted to doze off.

"Gregory Mick Adams, you will not use that dirty language in my house. Once in a blue moon, I'd like you to do something without me having to yell at you to get it done. I want you out of bed before I get upstairs or there will be major consequences."

I could only imagine what she had in mind. I can't even say freak'n without it turning into an international incident. I burrowed my head again trying to get back to the dream of Jasmine Alberta and me. She was doing amazing things with her Star Crusader powers.

Just as Jasmine Alberta was about to rip my shirt clean off my back, Mom tore the duvet off me. Thank goodness I had on my boxers because when I opened my eyes, my mother was standing over me like an unhappy drill sergeant.

I smiled a perfect smile that braces and her five

thousand dollars had paid for, but apparently that wasn't going to melt the iceberg.

Instead I got more grief, if that was even possible. Her eyes homed in on my smile. "Why isn't your retainer in? I didn't use my hard-earned money for you to have your teeth all shift back the way they were. Do you think money grows on trees?"

"Mom, I'm thirteen-years old, almost fourteen in ten days, seven hours, twenty-five minutes, and I think I'm old enough to know that money doesn't grow on trees. Jeez, give me a break."

I tried to grab back the covers, but she had been awake considerably longer than I and her reflexes were a heck of a lot faster for someone so much older than Jasmine Alberta. I was going to have to join a gym if my forty-year-old mother could wrestle a duvet from me.

"Gregory Mick, I'm warning you. You can have a quick shower, and not a twenty-minute one, and then a bite to eat. I want this room cleaned up, or I swear I'm going to do it myself and I'll be tossing more than I'll be keeping."

My mother morphed into a headless monster and I had to rub my eyes to rid myself of the horrible image.

"Mom, do you mind? I don't watch you get out of bed." I pleaded, trying to cover myself.

"That's because you're never out of bed when I get up. Oh for heaven's sake, I used to change your diapers. Get over it." She slammed the door, giving me the peace and quiet I wanted.

"Gregory Mick, don't think you're going back to sleep." My mother hollered down the hallway, the door vibrating. Then she did the worst possible thing. Even worse than pulling me out of my cozy cocoon, interrupting the coziness I'd been sharing with Jasmine Alberta.

She put on the CD player to the group WHOMP and began to sing—off key.

Music, she called it. Pathetic noise, really. It was horrible. You can understand all the words. It was plain yucky. WHOMP was so ancient that Mom originally listened to it on a record player. I know I had no idea what a record player was either. I had to check it out on the Internet, and it looked like something from outer space. Imagine not taking your music with you. I bet archaeologists will find one with the dinosaur bones.

I saw a WHOMP record at a garage sale, once, and Mom paid five cents for it. Told you—pathetic. I don't know what she'd been thinking. We don't even own a record player. That didn't bother Mom though. It's hanging on the wall in the dining room.

Some families have Jesus on the cross, mine has WHOMP on the wall.

Yep, not only did my mother curse me with the name of her pop singer idol with highlighted hair, I had to listen to him and his band at high decibels every time we were in the car. Yep, mom had an old tape player in the car, and yes, my mom had a mix tape, though how she could call it a mix tape when it was only one band, I have no idea. But hey, if you can figure out mothers, let me know, I think we'd be millionaires.

There was a fate far worse than death and yours truly was living and breathing it.

Chapter 2

I hopped in and out of the shower in record time, at
least for me. I wrote "I'm awesome" in the steamed
mirror. I ran my hands expertly though my brown curly
hair, knowing no matter what I did it would resort back
to the way it always goes. Mom says she would give
her eye teeth for my curls. Like what the heck would I
do with extra teeth? My mom is weird. With a towel
smelling of lemons wrapped around my waist, (not due
to me but mom's detergent), I headed back into my
room.

"Get me up before you get gone," I hummed. I
freak'n hated it when I couldn't get a song out of my
head, especially when it was WHOMP. "My heart
strings you play like a yo-yo."

I opened the top drawer of my wooden dresser that
for some strange reason didn't stick. I've had it since I
was ten and my mom found it at a garage sale, yep, the
same one as the record. What a treasure trove that place
was. I could never open the top drawer on the first pull.

Today it slid open, almost knocking me off my
feet.

I reached in, searching for some clean boxers, but
there was nothing inside. It was completely empty.

Who freak'n stole all my underwear?

I pulled open the door to my bedroom and waited
until WHOMP took a breath before yelling downstairs.

"Mom, where are my shorts?"

"Look on your floor. Isn't that where all your clothes are?"

Sure, easy for her to say. I couldn't see my floor for all the clothes thrown there. I don't know why my mom can't put my shorts and shirts in the proper place when she's finished washing them. It wasn't like she had a job or anything. One thing that dad was nice about in the divorce, giving us money so Mom didn't have to work. His major guilt trip worked to our advantage.

Sighing, I waded through the ankle-deep pile of jeans and socks until I found a pair of green plaid boxers and a Star Crusaders t-shirt. Okay, they were semi-clean. I threw on a pair of cargo shorts and I was GtoG.

Crapola! I knew I wasn't going anywhere until I dealt with my sty of a room. The drill sergeant had laid down the law. I still don't understand why I had to clean up my mom's mess but whatev. I picked up one of the shirts and grimaced at its foul odor.

GROSS! Yuck! Crikey, were all these clothes dirty? A few trips to the laundry hamper and I was free as a bird.

My goldfish's tank looked reasonably clean, so I fed her and went to grab some grub for myself.

I trotted down the stairs without a care in the world. My room was pretty decent except for all the 'dust collectors' that each had their special space. Mom had to understand. She knew I was a gatherer. I kept restaurant toys, rocks and comic books. In fact, that's where I was headed today. ComTol—the largest comic book fair in North America and it was happening in

Toledo.

I reached up and got a bowl from the cupboard and hauled down a box of cereal from the pantry. I poured the cereal into the black bowl, only spilling a handful on the table and a few circles of oats onto the floor.

"Lucky, come here girl." My Golden Retriever was my BFF. She ate all the food I didn't like, so I shared some I did.

The ringing of the phone interrupted the peace, startling me. I jumped up, spilling the rest of my breakfast on the floor, and while Lucky ate the evidence before Mom spotted it, I went in search of the phone.

You know how the phone is supposed to be in the cradle? Well, my mother happens to drop it where she was last. So it could be anywhere from the front room to the bathroom. More often than not, I've found it in the laundry room. Ever since Dad left, laundry was her life.

You try and figure that one out, I sure as heck couldn't. Just like we have to have a landline when it would be so beneficial if I had an unlimited cell phone; as it is I have to monitor my minutes. Mom says it's good fiscal responsibility, I say it's an excuse for her to make me do math. She's tricky that way. I'm working on my dad, my mom is a lost cause on anything other than laundry.

Just as it went to the answering machine, I located it, read the call display and pushed the talk button.

"Sawyer, don't hang up," I said, panicking into the phone.

"Hey G.M. are you going to be ready to go in half? My father is more excited about this stupid comic show than you. He's such a kid. It's so embarrassing,"

Sawyer said in his thick Canadian accent.

A recent transplant from Newfoundland, he tended to exaggerate his syllables when he was stressed. I have given up counting the 'eh's at the end of his sentences and sometimes I caught myself adding it, honorary Canadian, I guess.

Obviously he was stressed because it took him a whole thirty seconds to get that final sentence out.

"Yep, I'll just grab my wallet and I'll be waiting outside," I said.

"You're going to be waiting where and for whom?" My mother stood in the doorway, with a basket of clothes on her hip.

"Sawyer, I'll see you in half." I hung up the phone and gathered my strength. "Mom, you know what today is?"

"The day you get to bugger off to who knows where and I get to do laundry. Laundry that has been piling up since Hector was a pup."

"Who's Hector?" I asked, wondering if we were getting another dog.

"Never mind, I'm judging by the overflowing hamper your room is now clean and all empty plates, dishes, glasses and bags of chips are in their proper places."

"More or less." I grinned to show her that despite her odd behaviour I still loved her, especially when I needed a couple of dollars. I'd even put my retainer in for good measure.

I was relieved when she smiled back. Once again I was the golden child. It was really freaky, almost like she could read my mind.

"There's money for you in the cookie jar. Of

course, I know it's the ComTol Convention today. Have fun and be warned. Tidying your room doesn't just mean throwing clothes in the hamper. If I do an inspection and find a cursory job, you can bet your favorite comic book it will be in my hand and the garbage man will be making extra trips to pick up the bags."

"Mom, you're such a kidder. The room is so spotless you could eat off the floor." Which, of course, is kind of gross but I'm sure you know how mothers are. It seemed to be some kind of ruler to which mothers judged how clean things were.

Lucky started barking before Sawyer even rang the doorbell. I guess she was filled with cereal and needed to go out because as soon as I opened the door, she ran outside, jumped over a small wooden fence and immediately peed on Mrs. Shank's evergreen shrub.

"Hi, Mrs. Adams, that basketful of clothes sure looks heavy. Would you like me to carry that upstairs for you?" Sawyer asked. "My mom has a cleaning lady named Mrs. Jones to do our laundry. I'll get her number for you. She is kind of expensive, but I'm sure she'll give you a discounted rate."

Parents are so lame and naïve. They always warn us kids to beware, and they can be snowed by the simplest compliments.

He's really nice to their faces but when there's any spot of trouble anywhere, you can bet Sawyer has his hand in it. Of course, I'm always there and get in trouble as well, but he sure makes life interesting and fun.

"I'll remember that," my mom said, sighing deeply. I knew that sound and thought maybe she had

Sawyer pegged after all.

"Really, Mrs. Adams. You shouldn't have to spend your Saturdays doing laundry. My mom's at the golf club today while my dad takes us to the Comic Convention. She was thinking of taking me, but Doctor Rose's wife wanted her to go to the club instead." Sawyer paused and I tried to usher him out the door.

No such luck.

"Well, it sure is a nice day for a golf game," my mom said in a tone sounding to me like she either wished Sawyer would shut up or that she really wanted to go golfing.

I decided to help her out. It was the least I could do, since I was feeling on top of the world. My room was clean and my clothes would be washed and folded by the time I got home. I even forgave her phobia about putting them away in my drawer.

"Sawyer, my mom doesn't golf and cleaning is her life. Now, how about we get out of her way and let her do what she does best. The convention is waiting for us."

"Gregory Mick, Sawyer, can we please get going? Hello, Sophia," Sawyer's dad said from the open doorway.

"Hi Rex. Thanks for taking them to the convention." My mom dropped the basket behind the door and fluffed her hair.

See, I told you mothers were weird.

"Sophia, have you done something different with your hair? It really suits you," Rex Finnegan said, leaning against the door jamb.

"Rex, thank you for noticing." I watched my mother adjust her shirt, which when I called her on it once, she said it made her look thinner.

At least that's what she thought.

"Sophia, why don't you come with us? I could really use some adult company."

No, no, no, I crossed my fingers behind my back.

"Why thank you for the invite, Rex, but I really have a lot of laundry to do, thanks to Gregory cleaning his room."

Yesssssssssssssssssss. I uncrossed my fingers.

"Oh come on, Sophia, the laundry will be here waiting for you when you get home. Come on, grab your coat and let's go. My treat."

I glanced at Sawyer, who shrugged his shoulders. Helpless, I watched my mom disappear up the stairs in a flash. She was back in no time with a pink coloured blouse I had never seen before and *bright red lipstick*.

Had aliens kidnapped my real mom when she was upstairs? I wondered to myself, because when she came back down she actually kicked the laundry basket with *unfolded* clothes out of the way.

"Don't sweat it, man," Sawyer whispered to me as his dad was helping my mom on with her coat. "It'll keep him out of our way and we can check out the babes."

Babes? At a comic book convention? Impossible! I knew sometimes they had stars there to sign autographs, but I was only interested in Jasmine Alberta. I was a one-woman man—too bad she didn't know it.

Besides, Sawyer's definition of the babes would scare even the most desperate and lonely man.

Chapter 3

Brabora lumbered across the clay-like dusty floor of his cave dwelling, his four short legs carried over four hundred pounds of hard living. Pulling himself upright, he reached into a natural rock bowl carved out of a crevice and popped a pierce of quartz into his mouth.

When the mineral hit his nervous system, his blood pumped faster, his limbs spruced up and he immediately felt like a young alien, ready to take on the world, maybe even take on the remaining planets in the solar system.

But he wasn't a fool. He knew as soon as the properties of the rock wore off, he would again feel his age, and three thousand years of time was more than he could take.

Controlling Earth was the solution.

It ought to be easy. Humans were extremely short-sighted about what surrounded their solar system. They only looked on the surface of things, not what was underneath.

That's why the Earthlings couldn't find life on the other planets surrounding theirs. They didn't dig deep enough. If it wasn't right in front of them, under their single noses, displayed on their ugly faces, they were blind to it.

Under the clay-like dirt of Zorone, there was an

entire city of dwellers. Miner cars, quite similar to the ones that traversed through the coalmines on Earth, transported the reptiles through the planet with the ease and speed of a supersonic jet.

There were certain similarities between the two planets, though. That's why he wanted to take over Earth. The land above might be ruined, but underneath it was a smorgasbord of minerals and soils virtually untapped. The Earthling scum's technology was sorely lacking.

Ignorant Earthlings. They were traveling through space, building that ugly monstrosity of the Space Port to reach other planets, while Zoroneites already had control.

Brabora flicked his serpent-like tongue out of his mouth and stretched it into his left ear. Surprised, he heard a rapping sound on the rock that served as the entrance to his cave dwelling.

"Enter." He swished his tongue back into his mouth and turned to see who had enough nerve to bother the extreme ruler of Zorone.

"Master," Esoong said, his middle eyelid dangling in his excitement. "According to the bettlebug we put in the Space Port, a Russian spacecraft is set to rendezvous in a couple of hours. I need to be there. It would be like hitchhiking a free ride to Earth."

"Okay," Brabora said rubbing his front claws together while he stood balanced on his tail. Handing Esoong a small white piece of cardboard, he patted the younger reptile on his back. "Success be with you."

"Yes, Extreme Being," Esoong said, his eyelid twitching and fluttering.

"Esoong, calm down. I can tell you're excited but

this isn't a trip to Pluto. This is a serious matter. The entire fate of the mission rests on your young shoulders. Failure is not an option. We need Earth. I didn't want to mention this to you earlier, but we are running out of time. We're in short supply of quartz, we're running out of quartz."

Esoong's third eyelid retreated inside itself, no longer dangling. No longer twitching. "What? That's impossible. We got a pile from Pluto. We have an entire mountain of it."

The leader sighed deeply and strutted over to the wall of the cave where he picked up a rock from the bowl and another from a stone table. He held them up for Esoong to see.

"It's the wrong kind," Brabora said quietly.

"Leader, I thought quartz was quartz." His eyelid shut in disbelief.

"Esoong, suffice it to say it's not. The quartz from Pluto is Ronzon based, while Earth's is microcrystalline based. See the difference." He held up the two rocks side by side, the difference obvious in color and texture.

"That's what we need to survive. Ronzon doesn't affect our system. We need the microcrystalline to offset all the dust spiraling around Zorone. This is space junk, it is of no use to us."

"Leader, I'm in shock." Esoong had to turn his head to look, since his eyelid was still sealed shut.

"You're smart. I'm sure you've noticed the elders are dying at a higher rate than normal."

"I just thought they were getting old."

"You are so young. What are you, five hundred years?" Brabora held up a claw, not expecting an answer. "Well, they are old, but Pluto's quartz is

15

poisoning their systems. The other leaders didn't realize the difference in the quartz before it affected a great many of them. If we don't get microcrystalline into their systems before our supply from Mars runs out, we're going to become extinct." Brabora pushed his reptilian snout into the dry, dusty air.

"I'll do my best, Master," Esoong said, standing up a little straighter and flexing his shoulder armor wider.

"The fate of Zorone rests on your shoulders. Now go and bring home the quartz."

Chapter 4

Max Bombard felt like a kid on Christmas morning. He didn't know what he'd expected when he traveled to Russia to join their civilian space program, but a replica of the United States wasn't it.

His parents had grown up during the Cold War, and he'd heard horror stories of hotels without toilet paper and threadbare curtains, not to mention towels you could see through.

Things sure had changed. He peered out the windows of the Moscow Hotel and surveyed the awesome scenery. The Moscow Theatre was sitting regally across the way, its majestic architecture of columns and carvings announcing the talent inside its doors. On his next visit to Moscow, he was definitely ordering front row tickets.

A faint chime rang from the phone and he stepped across the plush carpet to answer it.

"Hello," he said into the twenty-first century apparatus.

"Good morning, sir. The shuttle will be here in an hour for your space ride. Please drink only water and consume the pill provided. You do have it, don't you?" A crisp, surprisingly British voice chimed over the phone. He never expected the Brits to have anything to do with the mission.

"I'll be rip-roaring ready to go," Max said, hanging

up the headset before the person had an opportunity to say goodbye.

He dressed in the blue space suit, which had been placed on his bed, and left the room, only to return a minute later. Rushing over to the bedside table, he downed the pill without the benefit of water. The aftertaste had him grimacing. He wished he'd taken the time to wash the bitterness away. He was heading into space, he could suck up a horrible taste. Impatient, he then ran down the stairs to the lobby, too excited to wait until the elevator arrived at his floor.

He paced, waiting for the pick-up car, and almost skipped out to the Audi as it pulled into the drive.

A heavyset man in a well-made suit stood beside the car, clipboard in hand, and held out his other arm, preventing Max from getting into the car.

"Mr. Bombard, calm down. There are certain aspects of this trip we need to warn you about."

"Yeah, yeah, I know. I read all about it in the brochure. I agreed to everything. I've signed your release papers and paid my money. Now let's go." He pushed forward against the arm and was surprised to find it stronger than a steel rod.

"Mr. Bombard, there are certain things we cannot, for security reasons, list in the brochure. They are last minute details and you need to be made aware of them for safety reasons."

"Should you be talking about them out here, where the walls might have ears?" Max said, only half joking, scanning the entrance way to the hotel, smiling at his own joke.

A man who wore mirrored sunglasses, even though it was the middle of the night, climbed out of the car.

"What seems to be the problem, Boris? Shouldn't we be on our way by now?"

"Sir, I'm trying to go over the final details."

"Let's be quick about it." The unknown "Sir" faced Max. "You can read the papers on the way. Get in."

Max did as he was told, but he didn't like it. He wasn't used to being ordered around, as the head of Bombard Mining he was used to doing the bullying. But he didn't want to screw with the opportunity of a lifetime. He could feel the effects of the pill. His limbs heavy, more relaxed.

He was pushed into the back seat of the car, and the clipboard was thrust into his hand. The man with the mirrored sunglasses positioned himself into the front seat, where Boris joined him in the back.

Max glanced through the pages on the clipboard. "I can't understand a word of this. They're all in Russian."

"Typical American arrogance. Did you think we'd do it all in English?" Boris smirked and elbowed Max hard in the ribs.

He tried to catch his breath and get air back into his lungs. Finally he spat out, "Hey, I paid hard-earned money for this trip. Money I'm sure the Russian government is only seeing a portion of." Sarcasm was his strong suit, as he rubbed his freshly shaved head. "Let's work together here folks." Business success 101.

The unknown man in the front let out a deep sigh. "The papers just say what happens in space stays in space. You aren't to go home and blab to the American newspapers about the trip. We have a reputation to protect. After all we were the first country to land on the moon," he said smugly.

"I thought we were. Neil Armstrong walked there,

didn't he?" Max said, realizing too late he could and would start an international incident if he didn't keep his mouth shut.

"Well, that's what your government wants you to believe."

****

Roughly five hours later all the preliminary tests were completed. Max felt like he'd morphed into a lab rat the way he'd been poked and probed. There were even electrodes hooked up to his penis, which wasn't the most comfortable feeling, especially when the woman doing the hooking was a Russian cosmonaut.

She could have subbed for the Soviet hockey team without pads, her shoulders were muscular, her blond hair was in a tight braid wrapped around her head and Max would bet his bottom dollar she could bench press three hundred pounds. Heck, she could probably bench press him. She scared him more than the bodyguards in the car.

Wires were attached to the outside of his suit and finally he was ready to ride the elevator to the landing port of the rocket. Max didn't even see what it looked like, as the group was shuttled from the brightly lit room through a long dimly lit hallway into the well-padded elevator.

Drowsy, barely able to stand, the female cosmonaut held him up. The elevator jerked to a sudden stop, and he lurched forward. Escorted out, Max caught a brief glimpse of the sunrise before being quickly whisked inside the capsule.

In his semi-conscious state, he was stuffed into a chair similar to an airplane seat, covered with a gaudy orange material. The inside of the capsule was only slightly larger than a telephone booth. Buttons lit up and flashed like a Christmas tree.

The mesmerizing light show was making him nauseous. The Russians probably wouldn't appreciate American barf in their pride and joy.

The female Russian leaned over him and buckled him in. "My name is Olga and I'll be your traveling companion."

Max inhaled her strong scent of cabbage and the even stronger smell of rubber. His stomach lurched in protest.

Don't get sick. Don't get sick. Don't get sick.

Finally, the wave that had come over him passed and he trusted himself to speak.

"So if we don't make it back are we supposed to populate the planet together?" he asked.

He started when he heard his slurred speech. "I'm assuming from the look of disgust on your face that means no."

A sudden jolt of heat seared him as the engines fired up.

"Hang onto your hat. I think that's what you Americans say," Olga said.

He turned his helmet sideways so he could see her out of his peripheral vision. She was tightly gripping the armrests. He copied her actions and for the first time wondered if this was a good idea. Could he really trust Russian technology to get him into outer space and back? Or would the ship blow up before they'd exited Earth's atmosphere?

Suddenly without the benefit of an American countdown, they were jerked in their seats. Olga pushed the flashing buttons frantically, which even in his drugged state, he knew wasn't a good sign. He grabbed onto the armrest, and then clutched at Olga's arm, which she easily shook off.

They spiraled through the atmosphere, up into space, the rocket spinning. Max turned his head and peered through the small concave window. They passed through a blanket of clouds, then nothing.

Then tragedy struck.

Chapter 5

Who would have thought my mother and Sawyer's
dad would have anything in common? I half-listened on
Sawyer's phone, as we each had an earphone in each
ear and while Jasmine Alberta (yes, she's an all-in-one
woman, sings, acts and I know she would bring me
breakfast in bed) played, I heard my mom carry on an
honest to goodness conversation that didn't involve
cooking or cleaning.

Plus she giggled.

I tried to remember the last time I heard my mom
giggle and couldn't. I mean, she didn't even laugh
when Lucky pushed the tip of a whipped topping can
and ended up spraying it across the kitchen. If a person
didn't find that funny, well they didn't have a sense of
humor.

Yet, here she was wearing *lipstick*, sitting in the
front seat of a Lincoln Navigator with Rex Finnegan.
Even stranger was that Rex was hanging on every word
my mom was saying.

Sawyer's mom and Rex had been divorced for two
years, ever since she was caught with the golf pro.
Apparently, he had been teaching her more than golf or
maybe not at all, according to my mom's friend, Mrs.
Aikman.

I elbowed Sawyer who was now singing very off
key along to Jasmine's latest song and nodded towards

our parents.

"So I was at the grocery store one day last week and a lady came in and cleaned them out of turkeys. She bought all fifteen we had in stock. I guess she was having a giblet craving," my mother said.

Now I don't get adult humor, but something in that sentence got Mr. Finnegan laughing so hard he almost drove the Navigator up onto the sidewalk. Go figure. I was going to ask my mom what was so frigging funny but decided to let it pass. There are some things a teenager doesn't want to know about his mother.

Finally when I thought I would throw up at the antics going on in the front seat, I saw the twin arches of the Downtown Convention Center.

Mr. Finnegan drove past the Center, scanning the area for a parking lot, and found one four blocks away. I thought for sure my mom would complain about the hike, or at the very least make a negative comment. Exercise was not high on her list of priorities. She once told me her idea of a workout was looking after me. I mean, how much work is that? You can't compare that to running the Ohio Marathon, now can you?

After Mr. Finnegan pulled into the slot and got his ticket, he slapped it on the dashboard. We all started to stroll towards the Center, Sawyer and I led the way. Mom and Sawyer's dad walked really slow, being old and all.

As we got within a block of ComTol the sidewalks became more crowded and we were forced to go single file instead of side by side.

There was a homeless person begging for money. His hair was straggly and his beard was gray, a baseball cap sitting in front of him. He wore a ripped t-shirt with the scratched imprinting from the last Toronto World Series. I stopped and peered in his hat and he had more money in there than I had in my wallet, so I passed by. Maybe he could use some of the money for a shower. He smelt like our recycling bin the time I put in a plastic milk bag and it sat in the garage during a heat wave.

Sawyer and I came to stand in line behind geeks dressed as comic characters. There must have been a sale on Mouseman costumes because there were more Mouseman than anything else. Some visitors used their imagination and I spied an odd Green Sabre as well as a hot Llama Woman, who Sawyer took a picture of with his camera phone.

"Sawyer, what did I tell you about using that phone for evil instead of goodness?" Mr. Finnegan asked what I thought was a simple question, but a new fit of giggles erupted from my mom. Jeez, I can't take her anywhere.

"Come on dad, eh, I needed a new screen saver."

"Kids these days," he said to Mom.

I watched Mom lean over and whisper something in Mr. Finnegan's ear. He glanced at me.

Great! She'd better not be telling him any diaper stories. No wonder she doesn't get out of the house much. She doesn't know how to behave when she does.

Sooner than expected, we got to the head of the line. I don't know if it was really that fast or if it was just because I had so many interesting things to watch the time just speed by.

My mom started to insist on paying for her and me, but Mr. Finnegan brushed the comment aside and said her money wasn't good here and paid with two twenties. As long as I lived, I would never understand adults. How come her twenty wasn't good here but his was?

Oh crapola, my mom had counterfeit money. How cool was that?

"Mom, is that a fake twenty? Can I see it?" I asked what I thought was a well-thought-out question. My mom is always telling me to think before I speak.

"Boys these days," my mom said to Sawyer's dad and had another fit of giggles, which I have to tell you was starting to get on my nerves.

Mr. Finnegan handed us each a ticket. "Don't lose the stubs once you get in the door. The girl at the counter said there's a special draw at five o'clock."

"Here Mom, you might as well take mine." I handed it to her and she promptly put it in her pocket. "I never win anything anyway."

Sawyer shoved his ticket in his jeans, then turned his back on our parents and elbowed me hard in the ribs. "G.M., look over there."

I glanced over to where he pointed. Several feet away stood the largest comic book I had ever seen in my life. It had to be at least twenty feet high by ten feet wide and it moved. I gaped as the thick pages shifted position every minute.

Mesmerized, I stepped over to the book. I joined the throng at the base of it, eyes wide, mouth agape. The vibrant colors streamed on the pages.

"G.M. isn't that the coolest? I think Llama Woman just lost her spot as my screen saver," Sawyer commented, tucking his long bangs behind his ears, as he took aim again with his phone.

I ignored him. In fact, the volume in the entire center dropped to a dull roar as I stared at the comic book. It was a new concept, a new series that Bombard Comics was launching.

Bombard was the hottest, up and coming comic book franchise. I remember reading a long time ago the owner was an employee at a rival company. He felt he was being treated unfairly because he'd booked his holidays and a more senior member wanted the time off, so he'd had to work. He didn't take too kindly to that, quit and started his own company. Ironically, he was now working harder than ever and never got any time off.

It appeared success paid off.

Max Bombard was the deity of the comic book world and he was here signing mini versions of the huge book. All I had to do to meet my hero was get in another line.

"Come on boys, there's lots to see and do here. This is only the first aisle," my mom said.

"Mom, every poster in my room is from Bombard comics and he's here." I pulled at my mom's arm like I was seven years old instead of almost fourteen.

"Gregory, I'm sure Mr. Finnegan doesn't want to wait around while you drool over Mr. Bombard."

"Now, Sophia, that's why we brought the boys here. Sawyer and G.M. have talked of nothing else for months. I've been *bombarded* with their enthusiasm," he laughed and, yes, my mother had another fit of giggles. "Anyway, why don't we let them wander around and we'll mosey through the aisles by ourselves, have some lunch and meet the boys back here at say," he looked at his fancy watch, "four o'clock. Then if they want to see something else, we'll hang around a tad longer then go and have some dinner. It's so rare I get downtown that I really don't want to rush the day or the pleasant company. Did you have plans for tonight, Sophia?"

"Just a date with a laundry basket." OMG, did my mother just admit to Sawyer's dad she dates her laundry basket? If I could crawl into the comic book, I would.

"Then it's settled. Right, boys?" I nodded my head, as I smacked Sawyer on the arm. He wasn't listening to his dad, his attention caught by a red headed girl in a barely-there bikini handing out issues of Bombard Comics. I don't think he even realized she had the latest issue.

"Sure dad, we'll see you later."

My mom opened her wallet and handed me twenty dollars. I thanked her, hoping it wasn't the counterfeit money and I'd be arrested, but then I remembered I was in the same room as Max Bombard and suddenly I didn't care if they locked me up and threw away the key. As long as I got Max's signature on the latest issue, I'd be the happiest prisoner ever. Well, I would be if they let me have with me what was soon to be my most prized possession.

I glanced at my mother. Her eyes were happy and she had a smile playing on her lipstick-ed mouth. She looked more relaxed than I'd seen her in years. It must be the atmosphere here at the convention that had done it. After all, who couldn't be content being surrounded by all the comic books and live characters?

Chapter 6

"How much longer do we have to stay in this place?" Yanking on his agent's collar, Max Bombard pulled the man closer so he could whisper in his ear.

"Maxxy B, you are scheduled to sign autographs until the draw," Jonathan Crawley said, jerking away and re-adjusting his collar.

Max Bombard might have had enough money for designer clothes, not to mention the fully equipped SUV sitting in the reserved parking spot at the Center, but the man should realize how he got it. It was thanks to his line of pre-teens who spent their newspaper delivery money on his comic books, who afforded him such luxuries.

Crawley surveyed the line snaking around the display unit waiting for the signature of a twenty-something year old. His gaze settled on Max Bombard, who's shaved head was starting to grow in, not a good look, and the clothes on the homeless person he'd seen on the way in were cleaner. Crawley wished he'd remembered to bring clothes for Max, maybe he could find a t-shirt at one of the booths, lol. Or maybe one of the Furrie's could loan him an outfit. He chuckled to himself, picturing uptight Max Bombard with kitten ears and tail.

Max clenched and unclenched his fingers several

times. "My hand is cramping and I have no intention of staying here much longer. I thought it was going to take an hour. I'm too busy to spend any more time than that here." His eyes surveyed the crowd in the auditorium. "I have big plans tonight."

He might be only twenty-two, but he was already in the Fortune Five Hundred Club. His popularity with the ladies knew no bounds. They didn't care if his clothes were clean, or he smelt, as long as he treated them well. Jewelry and trips to his private island always placated them.

Warriors from Pluto had surpassed the record as one of the most sought-after comic books of all time. The hype of the Warriors movie was causing a media frenzy no one had seen. Warriors from Pluto, or WFP as the trades called it, wasn't set to premiere for three years.

"Jonathon, I need a drink and I don't want any of your flower flavored water. I want a manly drink. Tell these punks I have to take a break and I'll be back in fifteen." Max got up, and without waiting for approval, left the stage.

He'd earned it. He ran his hand through his growing in shaved hair, the ends now highlighted, hair that cost him one thousand dollars, mostly because Jose came to his house. It cost money to look this disheveled. Who would have thought three years ago he'd even know a hairdresser named Jose? Let along have him on call at a moment's notice.

Life sure was strange.

The press said he'd left PaintleyComics due to a conflict in holidays but there was actually no problem other than he'd been bored. PaintleyComics knew a genius when they saw one and they'd treated him like a hero. He'd had his pick of offices, with all the perks any aging teenager would want or need.

His office had a big screen television and a computer hot off the assembly line. He had sleep pods, his own robot and five secretaries at his beck and call. He had it made, but like all geniuses, he wasn't happy. Something was missing. He felt like he'd drawn himself into a box.

So he'd handed in his notice, took a backpacking jaunt across Europe, and while watching the clouds form over Loch Ness, got the inspiration for Warriors from Pluto.

And he had rocketed to stardom. Now he had a house in Malibu where Pro Golf Players called him to go golfing, an apartment in New York with several Yankee baseball players as neighbors, and a real estate agent optioning him an island rumored to be in the same chain as Jason Montana's, the actor with the distinctive title of winning an Oscar three years in a row.

Go figure.

Life was good. So good in fact, he'd just returned from space three weeks ago. His life motto was, if you're gonna write it, experience it. When a seat became available on the Russian spacecraft, Volda, he'd gladly paid the over inflated price.

But what a trip! At least what he could remember of it.

The crowds parted for him like the Red Sea as he headed to the reserved room at the back of the arena. When he finally shut the door, he sneered. He was Max Bombard, and this comic book crap enabled him to travel through the Milky Way. The price he had to pay was he had to put up with the minions who lined up to see and meet him.

BORING!

His heart started to palpitate in his chest and his breath came in short pants. Max rushed to the back of the podium behind the curtains and bent over at the waist, trying to get a hold of himself.

He hated when this happened, and it had been happening more and more frequently since he'd returned from Russia.

Panic attacks.

Not your everyday run of the mill panic attacks that had been diagnosed by doctors and written up in books. In fact, when he'd gone to see the doctor at the urging of Crawley, he'd been laughed right out of the office.

Dr. Tom Bridge hadn't taken him seriously. He hadn't said it in so many words, that he needed a visit in the loony bin. He gave him a more reasonable answer.

"Max, my dear boy. You're stressed out. You've been working night and day trying to get this latest comic book on the shelves and you need to relax. Your body is telling you to slow down, take a break. Go on a holiday, get a girlfriend, enjoy life."

When Max asked if the Doctor could prescribe something, he smiled a sage smile.

"I just did. You don't need drugs to further complicate things, you need a holiday."

Max glanced over his shoulder to ensure that no one had followed him through the curtain and was witnessing his humiliation.

He reached into his pocket and pulled out the

powder. He licked his finger and stuck it into the little container filled with the matter and quickly put it in his mouth, enjoying the rush flowing through his veins. His breathing returned to normal and his heart rate slowed.

The doctor might think he needed a holiday, but he sure as heck couldn't explain why his body craved quartz.

Chapter 7

"Great, that's just my luck. When I finally get to the front of the line, Mr. Bombard goes on a break," I moaned to Sawyer who was too busy checking out the roller-blading girls, who balanced on one foot while handing out free t-shirts.

I didn't know how he could look at girls when *the* Max Bombard was breathing the same air as us. I don't think I'll ever figure out my friend.

"So, do you want to leave and come back? There's a lot of flesh, I mean fresh stuff to see," Sawyer said absently, watching the girl in the skin-tight mini skirt skate by us.

"You go and I'll wait here. He shouldn't be gone too long, and I can meet you somewhere," I begged. I couldn't give up on Max when I was soooo close to actually meeting him.

I was this close at hand to getting Max's signature and I wasn't about to throw it all away to have a girl who looked like she'd last eaten three weeks ago hand me a comic book or t-shirt. I knew how to prioritize, even if Sawyer didn't.

"Fine, I'll wait here with you. How about you hold my spot, eh? See that girl over there in the green bikini. She winked at me, not once but twice." Sawyer gave a little finger wave and she smiled back. "Twice I tell you. Once might have been in her job description, but twice, no way. She definitely has the hots for me. I'm going to go and get a comic and her phone number or in the very least her email address. I bet you five bucks I'll be texting her by midnight."

He held out his hand for me to fist pump, which I gladly did. I wasn't stupid. I knew she was paid to chat up the clients. If he did get an email address tonight, it would probably be bogus. He had as much chance of getting personal info off of her as I did of saving the world from aliens.

Some things just weren't going to happen.

I watched my friend stroll over to her and attempt to chat her up. She smiled and rocked back and forth on her roller blades. Was he making progress?

Sawyer lined her up for his camera phone and held it up so they could both be in the shot. He wrapped an arm around her and even I could see him smack her butt.

She frowned, anger blazing in her eyes and slapped him loudly across the face. A slap heard across the room. I didn't want to embarrass him further, so I pretended I was looking elsewhere.

Looked like I'd be keeping my money, but I might need to buy Sawyer some ice.

"So what happened?" I asked Sawyer as he slunk back into line beside me and silently handed me one of the comics she had given him before the slap.

"Stupid girl. How was I supposed to know she had a boyfriend? I'm glad she's not my girlfriend, smiling and chatting up guys getting them to take a free comic book and then when the guys are encouraged and offer a simple compliment, bam. All I did was say she looked really hot and then she slapped me. Stupid show! I oughta sue them." He rubbed the red mark.

It was all I could do not to laugh. I wanted to know how he discovered so much about her from a slap across the face, but just as I was about to ask, Max Bombard came back to the table and sat down in the middle chair.

Awestruck, I watched him pick up a bottle of water, drink it in one gulp, and beckon me over. Yes, I got a finger wave from Max Bombard. How awesome was that?

I thought I would be tongue-tied when I finally got face to face with him, but instead my mouth was going a mile a minute.

"Mr.Bombard,Ican'tbeleiveifinallygettomeetyou." I paused when his eyes met mine and he grinned.

He grabbed the latest issue of Warriors from the Planet Zorone from the stack beside him, and with a flourish of a marker I could smell across the table, he signed the cover and handed it to me. I didn't care how long the line was behind me, I'd waited for two hours plus his break for this moment.

He looked as great up close as he did on the Internet. He was the epitome of coolness. I wish I could get that bed head and wrinkled clothes look on purpose. I think I'd have to tell Mom to quit folding them. Probably wouldn't be too hard, she didn't like to put them away anyways. Or maybe that was me. Shouldn't be too much of a stretch. Okay, let's face it, I'd waited for this moment as long as I'd collected comics.

"Mr. Bombard, I've got to tell you what a huge fan I am of your work." I wiped my sweaty palms on my shorts. "I must have read Warriors from Pluto ten times. I actually bought two copies, one to read and one to keep. If I had of been thinking, I would have brought one with me and had you sign it. I can't wait to read Warriors from Planet Zorone, but I got to tell you there were a few mistakes in Warriors from Pluto."

I paused to catch my breath and from the scowl on Max Bombard's face I don't think he was very happy with me. I hopped from foot to foot, suddenly nervous.

Mom always told me honesty was the best policy, but I guess in this case it wasn't.

"They weren't mistakes," he said to me through clenched teeth. "It's called artistic equations. That's why it's called science fiction. Fiction as in not true, made up. Hello! Do you get it? It's made up. Why don't you get a life and go outside? You weigh two hundred pounds and you're what, fifteen?"

"I'm thirteen, almost fourteen," I corrected automatically.

A thin older guy, who up until now had been standing silently to the left of him, took a step forward and put a hand on Max Bombard's shoulder.

"Okay, son. Mr. Bombard thanks you for your interest in his comic books. We appreciate you took the time to come down here and wait in line for an autograph."

Mr. Bombard took another comic from the top of the pile and had signed it for Sawyer. After he handed it to him, he was autographing another one to a boy behind us in line, dressed as a Warrior.

"Okay, now where do you want to go? I can't believe we wasted so much time on such a frigging jerk. I'm so not buying another of his comic books," Sawyer said to me as he marched down the steps off the podium.

"Ummm, boys stop." A thin bony hand grabbed my shoulder and I turned to see the guy who had been standing behind Mr. Bombard.

I shrugged off the hand. Who did this guy think he was? My mother. We stopped and each gave a deep sigh only a teenager can pull off and waited. Sawyer took the sigh one step further and began tapping his foot. I didn't dare be so rude.

"Please forgive Max Bombard. He's had a long day and as you can tell the line-up isn't getting any shorter." He gestured and we turned to see the line snaking its way around the corner of the PaintleyComics display and out of sight.

"Well, you can bet we won't be the ones lining up ever again to see him. You can tell him my friend here started the first web site page devoted entirely to Max Bombard," Sawyer said pointing at me, "and he's not impressed by how he treats his fans."

"You're the one who started *Max Bombard, Warrior King*?" The guy asked as I saw a few beads of sweat pop up on his forehead.

"Yes, I did. And I get over five thousand hits a month, but I can tell you I'm going to close it down or in the very least take it off line for a bit and think things through," I said, picking up Sawyer's train of thought.

"Here's a Max Bombard pen." He reached into his pocket and handed me a pen with one of those floaty things inside that was a Warrior travelling from Pluto to Earth. "By the way, my name is Jonathan Crawley, I'm Max's agent."

"Mr. Crawley, I think you need a reality check. It's not going to change our mind that your client is a jerk by giving us a stupid pen which probably doesn't even work," Sawyer said.

Jonathan's eyes narrowed and he smoothed out his suit. "Fine, if you're going to play hard ball, hang on a minute."

"Don't be long. We're heading over to PaintleyComics. I think my friend here is going to change allegiances and he'll probably have a new web site up and running with the Dragonroach theme."

I watched Mr. Crawley retreat. "Sawyer, do you really think you need to be so rude? Let's just go. I guess Mr. Bombard is having a bad day, and I'm not removing my site. I'll be a Warrior fan until death."

He poked me in the ribs. "Shhh, here he comes and it looks like he's carrying something. See, it pays to be rude. We're about to hit the mother lode."

"Thanks for waiting, and here's a bag of stuff for each of you. Because you spent so much time on the website and got the Warrior name out there so much faster, there's a new computer game for each of you which hasn't even hit the shelves yet." He handed us each a canvas sack with the Warrior Logo painted on the sides. "Also, there's some extra tickets for the big draw and a toy ray gun which will be the must-have Christmas gift this year for the pre-teens. Happy now?"

I dug through the contents of my bag immediately. "Thank you, that is totally awesome. I'll play the game as soon as I get home and put a favourable review on my website. Mr. Crawley, umm, if Mr. Bombard was nicer to people it would save you a heck of a lot of money."

The older man rolled his eyes. "Tell me about it, kid. And kid, just don't use that gun in the rain."

"Why, is it so cheap it falls apart if it gets wet?"

Sawyer asked.

Mr. Crawley smiled secretively. "No, but let's just say it doesn't act as it should. You could end up with disastrous results."

Chapter 8

"I can't believe all the walking I did today," my mom moaned when we finally arrived home and she flopped on our black leather couch in the family room. "And the French fries I ate. G.M., I never eat French fries."

"You and Sawyer's dad looked like you had fun," I said, kind of absently as I started to look through the five plastic bags of comic books I got from the convention. In addition to the Warriors gift bag, it seemed like every major company was giving stuff away. Like a comic Christmas morning.

I was in heaven. Every sack had at least ten different comics in them, not to mention bookmarks, cling-ons for the windows. Pens were a big giveaway too. Who knew? And my personal favorite, potato chip bags with comic book characters on the packaging.

How cool was that? I was planning on checking out the Internet auctions to see if any of these collector items had been listed yet.

"He's a very nice man," my mom said.

"Who's a very nice man?" I asked, my head trying to get around the fact I wasn't going to have to purchase a comic book again for at least a week. Who was I kidding? I was addicted. I would be down at our local comic bookstore first thing Saturday morning, like clockwork, bragging on the loot I landed.

"Sawyer's dad." Mom continued the conversation.

I glanced at my mother, bewildered. "What about Sawyer's dad?"

"Never mind," my mom said, in an exasperated tone.

"Well, it was cool of him to pay for our extra tickets, not to mention taking us out for dinner at that neat place by the Convention Center." I continued to rummage through my treasures. "But maybe he felt he had to."

My mom sat bolt upright on the couch, eyes wide. "Why would you say that?"

"Chill mom. I only meant because of the counterfeit money you've been carrying around. Jeez."

My mom ran a hand through her recently brunette colored hair. My mom's hair changed with the seasons. Summer was blond, fall slightly darker, winter black with blond high lights and spring we were back to the lighter color. I didn't need to look out the window to see the season, just survey my mom's hair.

"I didn't have counterfeit money. What on earth are you talking about?"

She appeared puzzled, but I knew better.

"Mom, it's okay. I don't think the police will arrest you if you don't know your money is fake. They just ask you all kinds of questions downtown about who passed you the wad. I know all about it now, so you don't have to pretend anymore. I heard Sawyer's dad say your money was no good at the convention. It was fake."

"Oh goodness, it wasn't fake. It's an old expression." She grabbed her stomach and laughed. I haven't ever heard my mom laugh so hard. Giggles today, laughter today, were there two moons in the sky?

I heard the front door bang shut and the sound of running shoes thumped down the hallway. It could only mean one thing.

All heck was going to break loose in three, two, one second.

"Mom, what's for dinner?" my older-by-three-years sister Demi yelled.

Demi! How to describe her. Annoying and so much a pain in anyone's butt. She had bright red spiky hair, and freckles covered her face, arms and legs. She was weird. Any kind of sports she tried, she ruled. But give her a math question and major confusion set in. I couldn't figure it out. I mean how can you be stumped by math? It was so easy. Maybe mom should give her a phone she had to monitor her usage and count the minutes, but she'd finagled a phone from dad for 'safety reasons.' Don't get me started.

Plus she was on the computer ALL THE TIME. I would often see her with the home phone up to one ear, her cell to the other and hitting the keyboard.

Once I asked her why she phoned her friend to tell them to go on the computer and she said because she wanted to talk to them. Okay, you try and figure that one out. I sure as heck couldn't.

"Mom, what's for dinner?" she repeated, dropping her backpack on the floor beside the couch. She flopped down in the matching chair and began a tirade of her shift at WD DOnut's, a donut chain so popular that it was popping up around the country at a rate of two franchises a day.

I don't know if my mom was paying attention but I sure as heck wasn't. I let Demi drone on, her voice sounding like a mosquito buzzing. Annoying, yet if I swatted her she'd tell and I'd get in trouble.

"Demi, we're tired from walking around all day at the ComTol, so how about I whip you up some hotdogs and chips? I already had French fries today, but I'll make an exception. All the walking, I can use the extra starch."

"MOOOOOOOOOOOOOOOOOOOOOOOMMMM MMMMM, do you know what's in hotdogs? And don't get me started on the chips," Demi whined.

"Demi, give us a break. Besides, the chips Mom bought are trans-fat free. That's what it says on the bag, so it must be true," I said coming to mom's defence.

"G.M., you might not care what you put in your stomach, but I do. I plan on being on this earth a long time and you are what you eat."

"Did you eat horse manure, because you're full of it?" I asked, innocently.

"G.M. watch your mouth," my mom said. I looked over at her and I could see she was trying not to laugh. I think my mom laughed more today than she had in a long time. It was a nice sound, kind of like one of those wind chimes. Not one of those cheap tinny sounding ones, but the ones that were expensive, musical and really pretty.

"Mom I'm going to go and get my stuff out of your way." I looked meaningfully at my sister and her backpack, but she ignored me.

"Aren't you going to share your news?"

"What did drip boy do now? Did he win an award for geek of the year?" Demi asked, flicking some donut crud off her shirt and onto the carpet.

Like my mom doesn't have enough to do. Good

think Lucky was lying on the carpet and made a beeline over to the donut flake. Usually Lucky, our dog, would sit near me as I had a tendency to drop food, especially food mom cooked that was supposed to be good for me, which tasted terrible.

I'm not even going to go there. The food that is good for you tastes like crap and visa versa.

At least according to Demi.

Just goes to show if a person has trouble with something as fundamentally easy as algebra, they don't know much about anything else.

"Mom, do I have to tell her? She's just going to make fun of me anyway," I said, standing up with my loot bags.

"Come on crud boy, spill the beans. I haven't got all night. Stevie is picking me up at nine." She looked over at mom. "That's okay, isn't it? I didn't figure it would be that big a deal because it's the weekend and all."

Mom wearily sighed. "Just be home before curfew. I don't think I'll be able to wait up for you. I'm exhausted and heading upstairs for a nice warm bath before bed."

I took the opening mom had left by sneaking upstairs to my room where I had peace, quiet and no Demi. Lucky followed me up, probably realizing she'd get more food from me than from my sister.

Lucky jumped on the bed, turned around three times and lay down, right in the middle of the comic book bags. I shoved my dog off the pile and then pulled the books out of the bags one at a time, saving the best for last.

As I withdrew each, I put them in a plastic sleeve

and filed them in binders I kept in my bedside table. I was organized with my collecting, despite what mom might think. The binders were color coded green for PaintleyComics, red for Bombard and black for ImagineCOMICS.

I jumped off my bed, startling Lucky who looked up, then flopped her head back down and shifted onto her side. I went to my bookshelf over my computer desk and took down a gold-colored binder. I'd been saving it for a special occasion and it didn't get any more special than this.

I carefully removed the comic from the Bombard canvas bag. I slid my hand over the cover, a miniature version of the humongous one from the Convention, the *Warriors from Planet Zorone*, the telltale Komodo Dragons looking feverously riled. I held the comic firmly in my hand before sliding it into the plastic protective covering.

I had won the prize at the special drawing, the miniature version of the automated comic book that had greeted the masses as they entered into the convention hall.

We had met my mom and Sawyer's dad at the allotted time and we waited for the draw. Mom had pulled my ticket out of her jacket pocket and I dug out the extra ones Mr. Crawley had given us in the goodie bags.

I held my breath and prayed to whoever was listening I would never ask for anything ever again if I could win the draw. I didn't hold much hope though, I'd made other requests and they came to nothing.

Max reached into a big spinning drum, covered completely with Warrior logos and pulled out a ticket, handing it to Mr. Crowley to read out.

"Everyone have their tickets handy? Ok, the winning number is 764."

"G.M that's your number," my mom said, standing beside me but really close to Sawyer's dad.

She was right. We had the winning ticket.

I collected the book and went to pose for pictures with Mr. Bombard. I thought he might have been a little nicer. Maybe he'd just been in a bad mood before. I was trying to give him the benefit of the doubt, but he was as surly as ever. But I didn't care, no, not really. When I decided to sell this book, it would bring me a heck of a lot of money. Maybe pay for my first house. Or a car or maybe buy more comic books.

That's why I had to be so careful. It couldn't be bent or the corners damaged. Some of the buyers were very anal about these kinds of things.

I put it away. One day, when I had nothing else to do, I would use my tweezers and look at each page. I had to handle the magazine with kid gloves.

I sat down on my freshly made up bed. To be honest, it did feel kind of nice when you went into a room and it was tidy. I spread out the other stuff.

I sure was lucky and Sawyer sure was pissed.

He'd offered to buy the comic book from me for ten dollars and then was miffed at me when I said no. I really don't know how he honestly thought I was going to take ten dollars for something I could get one hundred times more on the Internet.

Really friendship only went so far.

"G.M." Demi blasted into my room. "Is the little boy still collecting his little magazines? Where's the Llama Woman comics? I bet you have them hidden under the mattress where you can look at them when you're having your Jasmine Alberta dreams." She came over and flicked my ear. I found that soooo annoying, which is probably why she did it.

"I'm so going to tell Mom you and Stevie went to the drive-in the other night and you couldn't even tell me what movie you saw because you were too busy kissing." I made kissing noises as Demi's face flared up like a puffer fish.

"If you so much as breathe a word to Mom about that, I'm going to pour nail polish remover on each of your Bombard comics. It won't be a pretty sight and besides we broke up."

I knew she'd do it too, my hands started to sweat. "Okay, truce. I promise I won't say anything to Mom."

"What won't you say to Mom?" my mom asked from the doorway.

Chapter 9

Monday at school I was the most popular kid. I was even more popular than Evan Maxkovitxz, whose dad was a spy.

Well, we all thought he was a secret agent and it turned out he was really just a professional chess player, so okay that one really didn't count. But I was more popular than Janice Howden who was on a commercial for bed-wetting.

It didn't take much to be popular at Hugh Jackman Public School. Our school wasn't named after the actor, though that's what the girls like to tell everyone, it was named for Hugh Jackman, one of the founders of the Underground Railroad.

Eighty families passed through Mr. Jackman's church, hidden in the pews on their way to a better life. When my mom took me to church, which is on our school property, I kept trying to pull the pew apart, looking to see where they stayed until my mom swatted me in the arm, which I don't think you're supposed to do in church. Hitting, I think, is one of the deadly sins. If not, well, then it should be.

I was at my locker when Janice Howden strolled by. She was color co-ordinated in pink with pink shirt, short skirt, pink socks, and pink bobby pins in her curly brown hair. Then she spoke and actually said hi to me. She's one of the cool kids on account of her acting career. Her smile is natural, no braces for this girl. I didn't answer her as I figured she was talking to someone other than me. In all the time I've known her, since Junior Kindergarten, she's never so much as said a word to me but today she did.

She was strolling alongside Mindy Maples. Mindy was dressed identically to Janice but in green right down to her green bobby pins. They must have called each other to discuss what they were wearing. Mindy had blond curls and smelt of vanilla soap. Then the weirdest thing happened. Mindy asked if she could borrow a pencil. Mindy Maples wanted one of my pencils. Well, I now had all kinds because of the Convention, so I took a handful from my pencil case and let her pick one. She tossed her blond curls, smiled a smile that would haunt a thousand of my dreams and said thanks.

Could today get any better?

Sawyer seemed to have gotten over his anger at not winning the comic book and was happily sharing in the adoring public feelings towards me by sticking to me like a rock. In true Sawyer fashion, he turned it all towards him and whenever anyone came to congratulate me about winning the special edition comic book, he would say he was there when it happened and he met Mr. Bombard. It was always about Sawyer, but today I didn't care.

Mindy said thanks to me.

My first class was with Mr. Cabot for History. He had his teacher sensors working overtime because as soon as he came into the classroom he zeroed in on me.

"I heard through the grapevine that Mr. Adams has some exciting news this weekend. Perhaps he'd like to share it with the class so we can get down to business and back to studying about the Underground Railroad." Mr. Cabot leaned on the wall, hands behind his butt as he waited for me to continue.

"Sure, Mr. Cabot. There's not a lot to tell. Sawyer's dad took me and Sawyer to the ComTol convention and I won a collector edition comic book."

He sighed. "Well, is that all? I thought from the buzz in the hallway it was the Second Coming."

"No sir, it's not the Second Coming of anything. It's the first edition of a comic book," I said, which caused Mindy to laugh.

I knew that once she got to know me she'd like me. It was all in the timing. I looked around and saw her twirling the pencil. I had a lot more where that came from. At this rate, she'd be going to grad night with me in June.

Maybe I should be thanking Mr. Bombard instead of dissing him. Because of my winning the contest I had a temporary access pass to the cool club.

I Was In and I didn't have to star in a bedwetting commercial.

At lunch I felt like I was in a parallel universe. I waited in line patiently for my French fries after telling five people, no lie, I didn't want to butt ahead of them and then when I got my lunch I stepped through the door to the cafeteria and the cool club called me over.

Mindy and Janice always sat at the table by the window because rumor had it the sun reflected nicely on their highlights, at least that's what Sawyer told me was the reason.

Anyway, Sawyer wanted me to sit with him, but the girls beckoned and like a sailor hearing the sweet song of the mermaids, I sauntered trance-like over to their table. But I was a nice guy. I waved for Sawyer to join us.

"We only saved one spot," Mindy said, flicking her hair out of her eyes, "and it's right beside me."

"I'm sure we can make room for Sawyer. He's an okay guy," I said as my friend dropped his Star Crusaders lunch box on the table and let out a humongous burp.

"Gross," Janice said, moving further away from Sawyer, and I don't think the intention was to make room for him. "Awww, he smells, too."

"I do not smell. It's called aftershave."

"Isn't it called before shave? You don't have enough hair to shave," Janice said, rubbing her hand along his face.

"Very funny," Sawyer said.

I know what you're thinking, with Sawyer's money and his father's contacts you would think he'd be part of the cool club, but apparently not. Janice and he grew up together and their families had had a falling out over some winery going bust so now they're not speaking.

The parents were polite enough, when they meet up at school functions, but the kids have been brainwashed and have taken it one step further. Between you and me, I think they actually like each other.

"So tell me what's so great about this comic book? When my little brother found out you won it, it was like he wanted me to get your autograph," Mindy asked, unzipping a plastic bag filled with cucumbers, carrots and green peppers.

I dipped a French fry into the clotted gravy and waited until I swallowed before I spoke. "It's the next installment of 'The Warrior Series.' It's not out for sale yet and even when it does hit the stand it won't have the mini story."

"Wow, that's fascinating," Janice said, not covering her yawn. "How old did you say you were?"

"Comic book collecting is not for kids," I said, incensed that she would even think such a thing.

"That's right. You should have seen all the adults at the show. There were probably more adults than kids," Sawyer said, punching Janice in the arm.

"Okay, so can you spell losers? They are probably Star Crusader fans who dressed like Captain Fish."

"It's Captain Dishburn. Jeez, some people don't know anything," I said.

"That's because I have a life," Janice said, stealing a French fry. Obviously, it was okay I could win comic books and order French fries but apparently it wasn't cool to go to the convention. I could tell my time at the cool table was running out like sands through an egg timer.

The bell rang signaling the end of lunch and we shoveled all our recyclables in the appropriate blue containers and headed to our lockers, me to get my two textbooks for the afternoon.

The novelty of my winning didn't wear off all day which shows you how little excitement we get at school. Even on the bus ride home, Mindy made room for me to sit beside her.

"Umm, G.M." She put her hand on my knee and when I looked down I saw each of her fingernails had little green flowers drawn on them. I thought that was pretty cool.

"Yes, Mindy," I said, praying to whatever deity

might be listening to me the bus didn't get to my stop before she asked what she wanted to ask.

"I was wondering if I might get a look at one of those comic books that are so valuable. I don't know what to get my little brother for his birthday and since he's into comic books I thought I might get a few ideas."

It was then that I realized how evil and tricky girls were. She was using me to get to my comic books.

What would Sawyer do? I could either tell her to bug off or I could string her along and see what I could get out of her for wanting to get something out of me.

What can I say? I decided to do the latter.

Chapter 10

"So how was school?" my mom asked when I slammed the kitchen door and rustled in the chip cupboard for, well, chips.

I paused and peered around the open door at my mother, grinning. I couldn't help myself. "Mom, it was awesome. The Cool Club asked me to sit at their table during lunch and Mindy Maples asked to come and see my comic books."

"Just don't show her your etchings!" My mom laughed, she was sure doing that a lot lately.

"That would be kind of stupid, since I don't have any etchings and I have no idea what an etching is," I said, with a mouthful of chips.

Mom shook her head and laughed again. She poured herself a glass of water from the fridge and that's when I noticed she was wearing workout clothes. She'd been exercising.

"What are you doing? Are you sick? What's with the fitness routine?"

She ignored my questions and asked one of her own. "Much homework tonight?"

"None," I said, showing more crisps into my mouth.

"No homework, or NO HOMEWORK?" My mom asked, making no sense whatsoever.

I shrugged and rolled my eyes at Lucky. By the

expression on her face, she didn't understand Mom, either. But then again, I was the one with the food, so her loyalties tended to shift.

I dug my lunchbox out of my backpack and put it on the counter for Mom to fill up for tomorrow.

After petting Lucky and giving her a potato chip or two, okay she got three, but they were trans-fat free so they were okay for her, I went up to my room, the dog nipping at my heels.

Lying down on my bed that I've had as long as I can remember, I glanced around my room.

It wasn't a baby's room, it was a boy's room.

A solar system hung from the ceiling, which was out of date since it had Pluto as a planet, but I always had a soft spot for Pluto, probably because it was named after a dog. I hoped the dog wasn't named after the planet, cause that would really suck.

The posters on the walls overlapped and depicted my favourite heroes—the Warriors and of course Jasmine Alberta.

The few gaps between the comics allowed the robin's egg blue paint to peek out here and there.

I had my room just as I liked it. My computer desk was actually an old door with the doorknob hole still there. I used to think it was really cool as a kid to roll up papers like a pirate's telescope and drop them down through the hole until I realized I had to pick them all up.

Putting a pillow behind my head, I crossed my ankles, suddenly deciding to kick off my shoes in case mom stuck her head in the door. It was nice she giggled so much. I didn't want to ruin anything.

I went to get the gold binder and brought it back to

the bed. I opened the lid and just as I was slowly bringing the comic out to have a look at it, mom bellowed.

"Dinner's ready."

"BRT." I snapped the binder shut and left it on top of my pillow. After dinner, since I didn't have any homework, I was finally going to spend the time and examine it. It was like Christmas morning and I had the latest gaming system.

The fumes from mom's famous tuna casserole filled the air as I pulled out my chair and sat down.

"You're such a pig," Demi yelled. "Mom, he just put a spoon in the casserole and ate off it. Major Gross. I don't want any now."

"G.M. where are your manners?" she asked absently as she began to dish out the food.

"Gawd, is that all you're going to say?" Demi rolled her eyes.

I waited until mom's back was turned and stuck out my tongue, ensuring it was covered in tuna casserole.

Smirking, I ate three helpings, then grabbed two chocolate chip cookies, twacking her on the head as I walked by. I ran up the stairs glad it was finally time to open the comic. I pushed open the door to my bedroom and stepped over to the bed.

The gold binder wasn't where I'd left it.

It was gone.

Chapter 11

Max Bombard's day following the comic book convention wasn't any better. He was fighting a bad sinus headache and his head was throbbing.

"Crawley, get in here and get me my medicine. What do I pay you for? You should know by now that when it's going to rain, I get a headache of enormous proportions," he yelled, carelessly putting his nine-hundred-dollar shoes on his five-thousand-dollar slate coffee table.

Crawley came into the room, his sneakers squeaking across the marble floors. Despite the expensive clothes, he was still a geek. He marched slouched over reminding Max of a hunchback.

"Here you go, sir." He held out a bottle of water and dropped two red pills into his extended hand.

Max tipped his head back against the edge of his ten-thousand-dollar sofa, tossed the pills into his mouth and swallowed a large gulp of water. Reaching for the remote never far from his hand, he clicked on the plasma television that sat on the wall over the gas fireplace.

He ran his hands through his now longish hair, amazed at how fast it grew, stopping at his temples, massaging to try and relieve the pressure.

It wasn't helping.

Nothing was helping.

Glancing at the television, he tried to get his mind off his aching head. Flipping around the channels he stopped on a PaintleyComics movie.

"Sir, you know watching this is only going to upset you more," Crawly said quietly.

Max threw the remote. "I'm a grown man, Crawley, even if I do make my living writing kids' books. I think I'm mature enough to watch a PaintleyComics movie without getting upset. Just because the movie houses see fit to make several movies of the PaintleyComics, one with George Clowley, doesn't mean I'm going to get upset."

"Yessir."

He grimaced as his head continued to throb. "Even though my comics are ten times better, the graphics are one hundred times better and the stories are a million times more interesting, I'm not going to get upset."

Max's eyes followed Crawley's movement across the room as he moved the remote and anything that might get thrown out of arms reach.

"Okay sir, but you have to remember when you're not getting upset that PaintleyComics has been around a heck of a lot longer than Bombard Comics and they have a bit of a head start in the movie making department."

"Crawley, how many times do I have to tell you? It doesn't bother me. Now go! Find something useful to do," he ordered. "Like track down that overweight punk who got my comic book. The contest was supposed to be rigged. I wanted, err, I needed that comic book for myself. Besides if it falls into the wrong hands, it could cause a worldwide disaster of epic proportions."

Crawley raised his eyebrows. Mr. Drama King.

"I saw that. You think I'm kidding. You don't know the secrets that comic book contains, and I've never been more serious in my life. We have to get it back before Thursday."

"Why Thursday, sir?"

Max shuddered, fresh pain erupting through his skull. "Because that's when the hologram comes to life."

Chapter 12

"G.M., come on. We have to take Lucky for a walk, and then you have soccer practice," Mom yelled.

"BRT. Hey," I yelled back from my bedroom, "any idea where my gold binder went? I left it on my pillow when I came down for dinner and it's not here now." My throat was getting sore from hollering, but I was in a panic.

"G.M., you have two feet, surely you can come to the top of the stairs instead of making your tired old Mom come to hear what you're saying. Now, what is it that's missing?" she asked, hand on her hip and annoyance in her voice.

The old mom was back with a vengeance. Well new mom was nice while she lasted.

"My gold binder I put my special edition comic book in is missing." I spoke slowly like I was talking to a baby. She didn't seem to realize how important this was.

"G.M., I swear if your head wasn't attached to your body, you'd leave it somewhere." She moved to the bed and pulled it away from the wall, with a strength Hercules would be put to shame. "What do you call this?" Mom asked, holding up the gold binder like she won a gold medal.

Well, I guess if I was going to go to that much trouble I would have found it, but why bother when

Mom knew where everything was?

I scooped my precious book off the floor and gave her a fierce hug. "Thanks, you're the best. Now if you could just find my Wayne Chain hockey rookie card, I'd really be a happy camper."

"I didn't know you ever had that card," she stated. "Since when did you start with hockey cards?"

I smiled. "Mom, I don't, but it's sure worth a lot of money and you can find anything."

Her lips turned up at the corners. "Very funny. I must say I am impressed by how clean this place looks. There is always room for improvement, but it's a start."

"Thanks mom, I tried." I silently willed her to leave because I wanted to get to my comic book.

She ruffled my hair. "Come on, you can look at that when you get back home. After we take Lucky out, you have your soccer practice. So let's get a move on."

Once outside, Lucky stopped every five feet to sniff and or pee. We strolled to the soccer field and word had already spread unexplainably to my team, okay it was probably fueled by Sawyer being on the team, that I had won the comic. So even though I let in five goals, I was still the hero. It was a practice, if it had been a game I would have been roasted on a spit.

When we finally got back home, I had to do the math homework I had forgotten I had. I don't know if it's just me or not, but I always forget I have homework. It's only when my mom checks my stupid agenda I remember.

So at ten o'clock, I was doing fractions. I was so brain dead by the time I finished, I didn't have $1/8^{th}$ of an ounce of energy to take out my comic book.

Instead I slid under the covers and turned out my

light. As my eyelids shut, I caught a glimmer of metal from the gold binder. It blurred in my sleepy state and then mutated into an odd shape.

I sighed. Jasmine Alberta was waiting for me in dreamland and she was more appealing.

Tomorrow would be time enough to investigate the contents.

I slid into Jasmine's waiting arms and into a semi-conscious state as colours swirled in the room and the hologram lit up.

Chapter 13

I went to school Tuesday expecting to still have my classmates in hero worship mode. Well, they were, but not for me. Overnight, Mickey Moore's grandmother's house had caught fire and he happened to be walking by, noticed the smoke, and dragged his grandmother out. Plus, he had the foresight to call nine-eleven and saved everything inside.

For some reason the kids at my school thought that was better than winning a comic book. WHATEV! I guess I don't have to tell you how fickle schoolmates can be.

At lunch, Mickey Moore sat at the cool table and while Mindy did look up at me when I strolled by, and I swear on the Bible or a handy comic book she winked at me, but there wasn't a seat saved for me.

I was back in purgatory with Sawyer.

"So how's the comic book, eh?" Sawyer asked. "Have you looked at it yet? What's so special about it? What's the mini story?"

"Hey, one question at a time. No, I haven't opened the book yet. Remember, we had soccer practice last night so I didn't get a chance." I unzipped my lunch bag and moaned when I saw my mom had packed a tuna fish sandwich. Now I wouldn't be able to talk to Mindy, if the opportunity ever did present itself, because of fish breath. No boy wants to have fish odor. Yuck!

I watched Sawyer bite into a chicken loaf sandwich. His maid was so cool. Too bad no one taught him to chew with his mouth closed. I always tried to avoid sitting across from him.

"So when are you going to do it?" came his muffled question again.

"Well, tonight is probably not going to work. Mr. Cabot is giving us that major test tomorrow and I have three on three hockey tonight. My mom keeps me in so many sports, I don't have any time to myself."

"Probably so you're not in the house at the same time as Demi. All you two do is fight," Sawyer said. He doesn't have any siblings so doesn't know how they can annoy you big time.

"We don't fight all the time. Just a lot of the time and that's because she likes to bug me so much. I don't do anything, I'm always the innocent bystander."

"Okay!" Sawyer held up his hands in defeat. "Sorry I said anything. So I guess tomorrow is the grand opening of the comic book."

"I can't wait. Do you want to come over and we'll look at it together?" I asked Sawyer, thinking he was my best friend and deserved the honor as much as the next guy.

Sawyer said, biting into his donut, then displaying to me the chewed-up chocolate, "Tomorrow it is. The world will never be the same. We'll be one of the chosen ones."

Chapter 14

"Crawley, any luck finding that kid?" Max Bombard pushed the button on the intercom that connected the screening room to the office. Crawley had better be in there working, he didn't get paid to sit and sun by the infinity pool. "He's a fat kid, shouldn't be too hard to hunt down."

"Crawley, are you there? Where the heck are you? How am I supposed to concentrate on the next in the Warrior series when I can't get hold of the hired help? Crawley, damnit!"

"Sir, I'm right behind you."

He jumped, startled by Crawley's voice. "Jeez, would you quit sneaking up on me! You're going to give me a heart attack. I'll be the only person to die from one at the age of twenty-two." He smoothed a wayward lock of hair. "Now did you locate that kid? I need that comic book back."

Crawley rolled his eyes at the continual impatience. "Sir, Rome wasn't built in a day. I'm tracking him. It's kind of hard when they handed out the tickets and didn't take any information down. Lucky for us, the press took a picture of you and him when he won the book so I'm just waiting for the photographer to get back to me. Or I'll track him through the website, if he didn't decide to take it down."

"Crawley, you have to be aggressive in these situations. Don't wait for him to call, you call him back now," Max Bombard screamed. "I don't want to see your ugly mug again until you have his name and address, or better yet MY comic in your bony little hands." Max paused. "Well, what are you waiting for?"

Crawley left the room and Max sighed deeply. Man, it was hard to get good help. Why was he paying him the big bucks when he knew he'd have to do the job himself? He pulled open the drawer of his desk and grabbed the small tin of mints. He popped the lid and ate one of the bite-sized rocks that had been hidden there. The quartz calmed him, soothed his soul. Crawley didn't understand how important that book was——no one did.

Chapter 15

My room was quiet except for the clicking of my Star Crusaders clock. As the hands lined up on the twelve signifying midnight, something peculiar began to happen.

Lucky began a low throaty growl and the streetlights outside the window flickered. I shushed Lucky, afraid the dog would wake up the others in the house. Mom would be mad. She didn't like it that I let Lucky sleep in my room and she'd be fuming if Lucky caused a ruckus.

If she had her way, the dog would be outside in the doghouse. Sometimes Lucky heard noises I couldn't, but then again she also dreamed of chasing squirrels. I rolled over and shoved the pillow over my head.

Now where were Jasmine Alberta and I? She was just about to reveal to me her superpower, a superpower that only we would share.

I was in that semi-conscious state. You know the one when your mom calls you to get ready for school. Not the one when you wake up and realize it's the weekend.

Lucky jumped off the bed and ran around chasing her tail. Then she froze and stared hard at the window.

Okay, even I found this strange. I glanced over to where she was facing and saw the shelf above my computer table alive with action. There was an aurora borealis. The Northern Lights of colours were emitting from the gold binder. It flew off the shelf and landed open on the floor. The Warriors from Planet Zorone slid up and out of the plastic sleeve where I had so carefully placed it. I had been so careful not to bend the corners now those same pages were fanning open, causing a strong breeze in the room., So fierce was the wind tunnel it was whipping my curly hair across my face, not an easy feat.

Lucy crawled on her stomach and pawed her way under my bed, whining. I could feel the mattress vibrating caused by her shaking.

Something was very wrong when my guard dog hid.

I covered my head again with the blanket, but curiosity got the best of me, and I lowered it just enough so my right eye could view what was happening.

The pages peeled fast, stopping at the white insert card which was placed in every magazine to order direct and save money.

This one was different.

This one was a hologram of the Warrior from Planet Zorone, Esoong.

The colours swirled and snarled, twisting in a circle faster and faster as the hologram took shape.

It began to enlarge until it was the size of a water bottle.

Lucky began whining, like she had to go pee really bad. I knew just how she felt. My bladder was ready to burst. I wasn't even on a commercial and it was like I was going to wet the bed.

I crossed my legs and watched in awe as the three-dimensional Warrior grew.

Fatigue overcame me and I settled under my blankets, confident it was a dream. That's what I get for eating before bedtime.

****

Esoong stood wobbly at first, enlarging, trying to get his land legs after being cooped in the comic book for so long. He wasn't programmed to be squished between the pages. He slung his gun flick across his shoulders and went in search of prey. He was like a bear waking up from hibernation. He wouldn't come fully alive for a few days, but he needed to get his bearings. He was somewhat drossy and was unable to leave his immediate environment., but he was Esoong and he was going to make his home planet proud.

He shook off his stiffness and ever so slowly the mist of vibrant colours surrounding him changed into solids. He was no longer a rainbow you could see through, but a living and breathing Zoroneite.

His long forked tongue jetted in and out of his mouth, in search of food. A small housefly buzzed at the window. Esoong's long forked tongue immediately darted towards it. The fly stuck to the gummy substance, not standing a chance of escape. He had to make due with Earth food until he could locate the quartz.

His hunger satisfied for the time being, he went in search of another type of prey, one that would feed another type of hunger.

Chapter 16

I woke up at seven a.m. for school, even before my Star Crusaders alarm went off. I dragged myself out of bed and opened the door for Lucky, who raced out like her tail was on fire.

Mornings like this were the pits, when I woke up more tired than when I went to bed.

I really couldn't understand why. It wasn't like I was up all night reading the latest Teenage ALIEN book or cataloguing my comics.

Then there was the strange dream about Zorone. That's what I get for pigging out on chips before bed. Mom was right once again.

After rummaging through my growing pile of laundry, I pulled on jeans and a Warrior's t-shirt my sister had bought me for my birthday or something and threw on a plaid shirt over the top. I plopped down on my bed and pulled on my socks.

Maybe it was going to be a good day. I found two socks that sort of matched and they were clean, though I was so tired I didn't realize until after they were on that one was blue, the other black.

Something seemed out of place, something weird, other than my socks, I mean. When I looked at my semi clean floor, I was shocked to see what was in the middle. What is it with that stupid gold binder? It had to be Demi messing with my head.

Not only that, the comic book was out of the sleeve and in the middle of the carpet.

If she's damaged it at all, there would be heck to pay. Mom was going to get the dirty details of my sister's love life big-time and I'd use my vivid imagination.

I cautiously put the comic back inside and even though I felt like taking a chain and attaching it to the bookshelf, I didn't have time. I just left it on the desk. I would deal with it when I got home. Sawyer was coming over after school and we were going to delve into the book's secrets together.

I took the stairs two at a time and slid into the kitchen. I couldn't resist. Socks and tiled floor, a deadly combo.

I gulped down the orange juice Mom had set out at my place and wolfed down the bacon and eggs. Obviously, Demi had left for the day or you know I'd be getting a major lecture about pigs.

"You look tired, sweetheart. Didn't you sleep well?" Mom peered up from her own plate of dry toast, her face wearing a concerned look along with a couple of crumbs.

I'd hate to get old. It means you can't eat anything good anymore. My mom thinks she's living life on the wild side when she has a bit of peanut butter off a spoon. Whoopdedoo. Good thing she wasn't there when I scooped some out with my finger, straight into my mouth, though Demi was, so it was so worth it.

"I had a really wicked dream last night," I admitted, grabbing another piece of toast and lathering it up with cream cheese.

"See, that's what happens when you eat before

bedtime. Your body doesn't have time to rid itself of the chemicals and energy-producing foods hitting your system." She sipped her black coffee.

"Mom, it was really amazing too." Mom raised her eyebrows, which encouraged me to continue. "It was like the comic book came to life."

"G.M., don't talk with your mouth full." Oh no, Sawyer's traits were growing on me.

The phone rang and I was saved from a further lecture. I reached behind me to grab the receiver. Seeing the call display 'Sawyer', I immediately said hello.

"Hey, G.M., it's Sawyer's dad, can I speak to your mom for a sec?"

"Sure." Wordlessly, I handed the phone to her, disappointed.

"It's for me?" she asked. "No one ever calls me this early, who is it?"

"Sawyer's dad." I shrugged my shoulders, my appetite suddenly gone.

"Hi, Rex," my mom sang into the phone she held with one hand and fluffed her hair with the other, as if he could see her as a silly smile played on her lips.

Geez, adults.

"Is Sawyer ok?" I pulled at her sweater, and she rudely slapped at my hand.

She nodded her head and mouthed at me to go and get ready for school. I got my lunch out of the fridge, tossed it on top of my backpack and went to have a pee and brush my teeth.

I know, I was in shock too about the teeth brushing. I was in a fog, though I don't know if it was due more to my best friend's dad calling my mom or the most realistic dream ever. Maybe my dreams were evolving? If I could dream this vividly about Jasmine Alberta…life would be more than good.

When I returned to the kitchen, mom was off the phone.

OMG, she was humming.

"What was that all about?" I asked, shoving everything that lay in the general vicinity into my backpack.

"I don't think you need to take Lucky's bone to school," Mom said, watching me.

"Fine, so what did Rex want?" I persisted, not liking how this was playing out.

"It's Mr. Finnegan to you and he asked me out," she smiled, her voice in shock mode. "Where are my workout clothes?"

Like I'd know! If mom couldn't find it, then there was no hope at all.

"You can't go out on a date, you're a Mom." I didn't care how lame it sounded, and it did, even to me, but I meant it. I was tired and despite eating a massive breakfast, my hunger had returned.

"Believe it or not, G.M., Moms are people too." She smiled and shook her head. "Besides, it's not really a date. I'm just helping out a friend who needs an escort to a dinner a client is hosting."

Great! My mom is running an escort service.

"When?"

"This Thursday, heavens that's tomorrow night and that reminds me," she said in a daze. Apparently I wasn't the only one who didn't sleep well as I watched her put the bread in the dishwasher.

"Mom, you just…"

"I know dear. I was planning on washing the bread." She giggled, placing her hand over her mouth like I've seen Demi do sometimes.

"Whatever! Mom, you sure are weird. You were saying something about reminding you."

"Right! I need to make an appointment for my hair and get a new dress. Gosh, I hope I can get an appointment for a leg waxing. So off to school with you, I've got stuff to do." She kissed me on the top of my head and started punching numbers into the phone in rapid succession.

Leg waxing! Next she'd be getting a tattoo. Though that would be awesome to have a Mom with a tat. I'd get a Warrior one, though maybe not, with the grief they've been giving me lately.

With my backpack and Warrior baseball cap, I headed towards the bus stop.

It was a good thing my feet knew where I was headed because my mind wasn't up to the task. Between the antics in my room with the gold binder mysteriously moving about and my mom acting all girly, I needed peace and quiet. Hopefully I'd get that from school. I knew it would be impossible on the bus. My age group wasn't bad, but the younger kids all thought it was party central.

A massive headache pounded in my head. Great! Now I was tired and hungry with a throbbing head. I knew I just had breakfast, but hey, I was a growing boy.

The bus unloaded and the bell rang. I headed to my locker and whipped the dial around. The lock gave and I threw my backpack and cap inside. I grabbed my pen and the notebook I'd need for first class and strolled towards homeroom.

"Did you know your dad called my mom?" I whispered to Sawyer as the last bars of the National Anthem finished.

"Yeah, he has a client taking him out to that new fancy restaurant so he thought your mom might like to go." Sawyer yawned.

How could he yawn when my mom was so excited she was getting her hair done and likely her legs waxed? I shuddered. There were some things a teenage boy just didn't want to think about.

But still, it must really be important for her to go through that much pain. She'd told me once it was like having a bandage removed over and over again. I shivered.

"Hey, how about I come over when they go out? We can order in pizza and crank call Mindy?" Sawyer asked, turning around as the supply teacher rapped a ruler on the desk.

Finally things were going my way. At school, it was an easy day. The instructors were on some kind of holiday so we had fake teachers for every class and that meant we watched movies for the entire day.

The first period it was fun, but by the end of school, I was bored out of my skull. I mean, seeing a movie in French loses its excitement fast even with the girls in class passing notes.

Sawyer gave the bus driver a note to say he could get off at my house, which looked forged to me, but hey if the driver didn't care, I wasn't about to say anything.

We went through the backdoor of my house, which is always unlocked, and headed directly into the kitchen. Mom left a note propped up against the toaster. Sawyer snapped it up and read it. We had no secrets as far as he was concerned.

"Dear son," he read in a high falsetto voice. "I got in with Nicole for hair and legs. Will see you when I get home. Heat up some pizza if you get hungry. Love mom." He smirked.

"No wonder you're so honest. Your mom's signature is extremely hard to forge. Now what can I eat? I'm starving." Sawyer rustled through the fridge looking for anything unhealthy.

"Doesn't your mom believe in junk food?" Sawyer mumbled from inside the fridge.

"She does, but you have to remember who my sister is. Demi doesn't believe in any kind of bad food. Which is kind of surprising when you realize where she works. But she says she doesn't have to eat the food. Whatever!" I rolled my eyes. Sisters. "She's weird."

"She might be weird, but she's kind of hot," Sawyer admitted, shutting the refrigerator door and looking at a picture of Demi and Lucky. A milk magnet held it and she was in her work uniform.

"Major grossness! That's my sister you're talking about." I gagged.

"Your sister who looks like Jasmine Alberta."

I groaned and grabbed the sides of my head. "You have so ruined that fantasy for me. I'll never be able to think of Jasmine Alberta in the same way again. Thanks for that image."

I knew now I would have to rip down her poster.

"Okay, I'm set. Are you ready to go and do the dirty deed?" Sawyer asked as he piled a couple of cans of soda on top of the box of Ding-a-lings.

They were my mother's one weakness. Apparently during a certain time of month she has to eat chocolate.

I don't know about that because it seemed like every day she was pigging out on a Ding-a-ling. Oh well, who was I to complain, even when Demi complained it fell on deaf ears.

"We can eat more when we finish. Mom won't be home for quite a while."

We climbed the stairs, with me following Sawyer. I saw him sneak a peek in Demi's forbidden zone, before we walked into my room. Lucky came in just as I closed the door.

The pop fizzed as we opened the cans just that little bit that teens love to do and parents for some reason find really annoying, and we sipped from the cans as only teens can.

Sawyer squeezed the plastic bag with the Ding-a-lings and the cake shot across the room right into Lucky's mouth. She wolfed it down and sat salivating on the carpet waiting for me.

"Okay, where is the Holy Grail?" Sawyer asked, opening another package, with a lot more care than the last one, much to Lucky's disgust.

Pulling down the gold binder I then rustled in my bedside table for my surgical tweezers. They were not your run of the mill tweezers—Mom had got them from a friend of hers who worked at the hospital. I just hoped they weren't going to be missed in some open-heart surgery. But whatever. I'm sure they had more than one set.

I stepped to the bed and handed the binder to Sawyer who dropped it on the bed, more interested in licking the Ding-a-ling cream out of the plastic than in the comic book.

How could we even be friends? Sometimes I did

wonder.

Just as I was ready to open it, the backdoor slammed shut, and Lucky scratched at the bedroom door to be let out.

"Mom, I'm home," my evil sister, who so did not in the least look like Jasmine Alberta, called out.

Sawyer shoved the plastic from the Ding-a-ling under my pillow and wiped his mouth. Needless to say, I was surprised by his actions. This is the guy who used to brush his teeth once a week and that was on Sunday before church.

"Demi, Mom's not here, just me and Sawyer. Let Lucky out," I screamed back down the stairs as I went and leaned over the railing.

"What is that little turd doing in our house?" Demi came into my room and Sawyer grabbed the plastic from under the pillow, made it into a ball and flung it at her. It fell half heartily on the side of the bed.

"Did you hear what your sister called me? See if I share with her the money I got for her undies on the internet," Sawyer said in a loud voice, winking at me to show he was kidding. I think.

Demi rushed towards him faster than I'd ever seen her move and that was saying something. Her best friend called a couple of months ago to tell her that one of the singers from Billy Tenent was at the mall and she ran upstairs got dressed, make-upped and was out of the house in two minutes flat.

She flew over to the bed and started thumping Sawyer. She was having a pillow fight without the pillow. He was getting the heck beat out of him by someone who weighed at least eighty pounds less than him. And the worst part was he seemed to be enjoying it.

GROSS!!!

At least he was laughing.

I think she would have kept throttling him until the middle of next week, except he was saved by the ringing of the phone. She gave him one final smack across the head, then jumped off the bed and ran like a sprinter to answer it.

"I think your sister likes me," Sawyer said, rubbing an arm that was beginning to turn red.

"Yeah, I'd say so. It's a good thing she doesn't love you or you'd be six feet under. Now are you ready to check out the hottest comic book this side of Hades?" I said.

"G.M., you're wanted on the phone," Demi yelled.

"Okay, I hear you. Sawyer, who could be calling me? The only one who calls me is you and you're here." I slid down the banister hoping it wasn't a telemarketer. Demi entered a contest once in the hopes of winning a car even though she wasn't old enough to drive. She put down my name as her parent so mom wouldn't find out and ever since I've been getting phone calls trying to sell me everything from vacuums to trips to Florida. I thought the trip south would have been great, but when mom found out she put the kibosh on it. Once again, she was a major fun ruiner.

"Hello," I said, out of breath.

"Is this Gregory Mick Adams?" A deep voice resonated through the phone line.

"Yes it is, and I don't want any." That's what Mom said for me to say when these people called. I was annoyed. They always called at the worst time.

"But you don't even know what I'm selling, and in

fact, I'm not selling anything. I have something for you."

"For free?" I asked, in disbelief because Mom always said nothing in life was free and so far she'd been proven correct.

"Well, it's more of a trade. I have the latest gaming system which I'd be willing to give you in exchange for something."

"The latest gaming system? That would be fantastic. What would you like? I'd be willing to trade my sister," I said, only half kidding.

"My boss wants that comic book you won at ComTol, and we'll give you the system for it," he said in a voice that didn't encourage debate.

"That's really tempting but I haven't even opened the mag yet. So thanks, but no thanks."

"Wait, before you hang up. How about I sweeten the offer and give you an entire collection of games plus the game console?"

I could tell he was desperate from the tone of his voice, but I figured if he was going to give me that right off the bat, then I could probably get a heck of a lot more than on the internet, that's if I decided to sell. A comic book like this is only going to go up in value. If I played my cards right, I might have enough for a college education or maybe a Corvette. Then I bet Mindy would save me a seat at lunch.

"Kid, you should give me that comic book. If you know what's good for you. You're going to be sorry," the man said in a menacing tone.

I recognized the voice but couldn't place it.

"That sounds like a threat," I said, only acting brave because this jerk was on the other end of the phone and not in my house.

"Punk, that's not a threat. It's a promise."

Chapter 17

I don't know what got into Sawyer, he'd been to my house a gazillion times for dinner, but tonight he had good posture, and kept his mouth closed. Like through the whole meal. He never said a word. He even set the table without being asked. I hope my mom was too wrapped up in her social life to notice or I would be compared to Sawyer. Sawyer did this, Sawyer did that. I did not need the grief.

I didn't get a chance to tell him about the phone call, cause Mom came home with pizza and I don't know about you, but even when you're not hungry and you smell pizza, you have to eat it.

I knew Demi watched me with disgust as I inhaled the pizza, while she sat like a rabbit nibbling on carrots and a plate of lettuce.

"Just one bite won't kill you. You know you want to," I teased her.

"Mom, tell him to get it out of my face," Demi gagged.

"Gregory, get that out from under your sister's nose," Mom repeated in a robot-like voice.

"Mom, what's gotten into you? You couldn't care less that G.M. is trying to kill me," Demi whined.

"Didn't you hear the latest? Mom has a date." I rolled my eyes, much in the way that Demi and Mom taught me, but I think I did a better job.

"Mom does not have a date. She's too old to date. Now getting back to me…"

"Sawyer's dad called and asked her out for dinner. If you weren't so self-centered, sis, you'd notice her hair was just done."

She pinned our mother with a death stare. "What is that dweeb talking about?"

"Your brother is not a dweeb. Sawyer's dad called and asked me to accompany him to a dinner. I said yes. You're baby-sitting your brother tomorrow, by the way." Mom flicked her newly highlighted tresses over her shoulder.

"Mom, it would have been nice of you to ask me and not just assume I'm available to look after the baby. I have to work, so I can't."

"Mom," I said, disgusted. "I am not a baby. I don't need someone, especially HER to look after me. I'm old enough to be by myself. Besides, Sawyer said he'd come over." I looked at Sawyer for confirmation and he nodded, turning red as all eyes were on him. What has gotten into him?

"I don't know. I'm not sure how late we're going to be, and I don't want you two to get into any mischief while I'm gone." Mom chewed her lower lip. "Maybe I should just phone Rex and cancel." She looked sadly at the phone.

"Mom, we'll be fine." I thought I was the pro at guilt trips, but apparently not so. "Take your cell and if I have any questions or problems I can just call," I said, sneaking Lucky a piece of meat.

She brightened. "Well, okay, if you're sure. Now Demi, I want you to come straight home from work tomorrow night. No going over to anyone's house."

"Great! My mom has a better social life than I do. How pathetic is that. No offense, Mom." Demi jumped up and carried her plate towards the sink, but just left it on the counter instead.

"Umm sis, that plate is not going to clean itself. You can't put carrots in the dishwasher," I said joining her at the sink where I rinsed my plate off. I usually did as she was doing, but I wanted to make an impression on Mom so she would leave me alone tomorrow.

"Sucking up doesn't become you." Demi elbowed me in the ribs and I've got to tell you, it hurt. I bent over trying to catch my breath, admittedly putting on a show for Mom.

Sawyer brought over his plate, cup and used napkins and disposed of everything where they belonged.

"Sawyer, you were raised right." Mom stood and placed her hands on her hips, turning towards my sister, scowling. "Demi, apologize to your brother. He doesn't deserve to be sideswiped by you. He was just putting his plate away, trying to help me. Which is more than I can say for you. You make work for me!"

"Sure, you always take his side. He always has been the favoured child. I didn't know why you had me to begin with. You should have just skipped me and had him." She picked up her plate, slammed it against the side of the garbage can, the carrots falling onto the floor. Lucky rushed over to investigate and trotted back to my side when she realized it was something healthy. Lucky wasn't my dog for nothing, and I didn't even train her to behave that way. Pure instinct.

"Demi, how about you go and get ready for work?" my mom asked quietly. I don't know what it's like in your house but when my mom talks quietly it's worse than when she's yelling and slamming things across the floor.

"Fine, I'll go. Don't expect any donuts tonight." She stormed through the kitchen and stomped up the stairs. I held my breath waiting for the door and then it slammed.

"Anything else I can do to help you, Mom? Want me to make my lunch for tomorrow?"

"I've already got it done. I didn't want to leave it for you to do. Last time you made it, you put in trail mix."

I shrugged a shoulder. "So it was an accident."

"An accident that had everyone from the principal on down phoning and lecturing me on the horrors of taking peanuts into the classroom."

"Well, no one died, though it was kind of neat to see someone use an epi pen."

My mom paled.

"I'm only kidding. I didn't even open the container. The principal just called to make sure it didn't happen again."

I was silenced by the sound of Demi stomping her feet down the stairs. "I'm going to work, if anyone cares."

"Bye and thanks for dinner Mrs. A," Sawyer said, as he left through the back door.

"Goodbye, sweetheart," Mom called out as the front door slammed shut.

She stared at the path Demi had just taken. "Gregory, never become a teenage girl."

"Don't worry, there's no chance of that happening. We're going upstairs to do my homework."

****

Demi turned her phone on and turned it up to full blast, losing herself in the music. How horrible!! Mom going on a date with Sawyer's dad, if they got married, she'd have another annoying brother.

Silently she put her phone into her work locker, examined her hair and make-up and headed to the counter where she checked the coffee pots.

Whether it was her mood or the full moon, the customers who kept popping to WD DOnuts were annoying. One woman who needed to go on a major diet stood for ten minutes trying to decide between the chocolate crème-filled or the chocolate strawberry-filled before deciding to take both. Demi bit her tongue, trying to keep her comments and temper to herself.

The next customer denied ordering a large coffee when she'd poured it, claiming it was supposed to be a medium and since she had it done already, he should get a large for a medium price.

It was enough to make her lose her mind or at the very least binge on a donut roll.

Her beige uniform was covered with sugar dust when she glanced up at the clock and saw it was nearly quitting time. WD DOnuts closed at midnight and it was eleven fifty-five.

Swiftly she wiped the powdered sugar off her outfit and glanced up to see a burly construction worker pull open the door. He strolled to the counter and stood looking at the sign like it was written in a foreign language.

"I'll take twenty coffees—all double creams and double sugars." He yawned without covering his mouth, allowing Demi to see a tongue covered in fur.

She was smart enough to ring in the coffee before she began to process the order.

Syd, the baker, came out from the back and began carrying the emptied donut trays into the kitchen.

"Wait, I said twenty single creams and single sugars," he said, yawning again.

"Sir, you said double for both. I know what I heard." Demi stood up for herself. It had been a long frigging night and she still had a pile of homework to get through.

"Lady, I want the coffee the way I want it, not the way you want to make it." He fingered a suede tool belt.

"Is there a problem?" Syd asked coming in from the back.

"No problem at all. I'm just making this GENTLEMAN his coffee." She poured the coffee into each of the cups and even though she wasn't supposed to use the last inch of coffee, she used the dredges on the bottom of each of the pots, she was so ticked off with the jerk. These people who didn't have a life and assumed she didn't have one either really ticked her off.

She stuffed each of the cups into the cup holder and piled each one on top of the other. Surely if he could handle a nail gun, he could balance the trays.

"Here you go, sir, let me get the door for you." She flipped open the walk-through at the counter and rushed over to the door. Grunting, he walked through and key fobbed the blue van, the door on the passenger side sliding open.

"Demi, you look like you swallowed a lemon." Syd laughed when she returned inside. Syd was forty years old and just out of rehab. At least that was the rumor.

Someone wasn't quite normal somewhere along the line when they wanted to bake donuts till three am.

"Mother issues!"

"Okay, enough said there." He held up his hands in defeat.

After mopping the floor, she set about wiping out the donut trays, and then rinsed out the coffee pots, scrubbing the black muck out of the bottom. Personally she couldn't see how anyone could like coffee. It smelled horrible and tasted even worse. The only way it was halfway decent was if there was a gallon of sugar in it and that was just not acceptable.

"Bye, Syd, see you tomorrow." Demi searched her purse for her phone, instead finding her retainer case before finally feeling the smooth plastic at the bottom. After removing it, she pushed her phone earpiece into each ear and hit the play button as Billy Tenent's raw voice screamed into her ear.

She sauntered the three blocks south towards home, then turned at the Chy Convenience store and began to stroll the last two blocks.

She didn't even want to think about the homework awaiting her. It was her own fault, well actually, G.M. was to blame. Who could think about homework when his creepy friend was in the house? Awww, she was afraid that he did take her undies and put them on the internet. That was just the type of totally gross thing he would do.

She sang along with her favorite band, totally unaware of her surroundings. She was thinking algebra when suddenly she was grabbed from behind.

A clammy hand clamped down on her mouth, her phone went flying out of her ear and she was thrown to the ground. Her uniform was torn and as she struggled for air to fill her lungs, she was rewarded with a smack across the face.

Her face stung with a burning sensation. She kicked, trying to get purchase against her assailant. She scratched and clawed, thinking if she did die at least there would be DNA under her fingertips. The sweaty smelly hand remained clasped on her mouth.

"Calm down, I'm not going to hurt you." She opened her eyes and saw the construction worker. "I have a message for your brother. Tell him if he wants to keep his family safe, leave the comic book at the school yard at midnight tomorrow."

"Hey, what's going on over there?" a voice called out.

Demi rolled over and lying in a fetal position alternated between crying and sobbing, trying still to get oxygen into her lungs.

"Remember what I said," he hissed. "Go to the cops and your brother is dead meat!" Her attacker clipped her once more across the face and ran off down the street as Sawyer came upon her.

"Demi, is that you? I'm sorry. I know you don't get much action so I'm sorry if I interrupted a moment between you and your boyfriend." Sawyer turned to go, tossing his water bottle into his other hand.

"Sawyer, please help me. You saved my life," she said as she sat up only to throw up on her phone and the grass.

"Demi, what happened?" Sawyer eyed her warily.

Her humiliation mounted as she continued to retch on the grass. Whatever few carrots she'd managed to get down had left her now.

When she was done, Sawyer reached a hand out and pulled her to her feet.

"You stopped me from being raped or worse. You are my rescuer. How can I ever thank you?" She reached up and hugged him. She'd never been so happy to see the little creep in her life.

"Umm, you could probably help me by not squeezing the life out of me when you smell like barf, but it's the thought that counts. Now tell me what happened? Do you want to go to the police? I think we should call them." He pulled out his cell phone.

She grabbed his water bottle, gulped, and swished it around to get the taste out of her mouth. Spitting it out, she swallowed some, easing the dryness out of her throat.

"I'm fine. I just want to go home and have a hot shower. I don't think there's any point in going to the police, and it wasn't Stevie. We broke up." she said firmly.

"Did the creep say anything to you?" Sawyer asked, pushing her hair off her face.

"He said something strange about G.M.'s comic book. What is so damned special about that book?"

"I really don't know. We opened it and there was nothing in it that wasn't in a regular book. I was disappointed, but after meeting that jerk Max Bombard, I wasn't surprised."

"Okay, I've had enough about that darn comic book. The guy said Gregory was supposed to take it to the school yard tomorrow at midnight."

"You mom is going out with my dad and G.M. and I are going to be alone. I don't want go to school, especially at night."

She brushed herself off, and after picking up her phone from the grass, she rushed towards home.

Turning around, she saw Sawyer standing there. "Well come on. What are you waiting for? I wouldn't mind some company." She waited for him to join her, and then she linked her arm through his. "Sawyer, if you tell G.M. I said this I will deny it until the day I die, but I'd like to thank you for helping me." She learned over and kissed him on the cheek.

"I promise I won't tell," Sawyer said, glad it was dark and she couldn't see him blushing.

"And Sawyer, about my underwear showing up on the internet?"

"I swear I wasn't going to do it. I was only bugging you about doing it."

"It doesn't matter. But no more."

"I.... oh never mind. You don't believe me anyways. And you did kiss me."

"Sawyer!!!!!"

He learned over and kissed her right on the lips.

"Don't push it," she grinned. He did know how to lay on an impressive lip lock. "How did you learn to kiss so well? With your pillow?" This boy could teach a lesson at high school.

"I'll never tell, but you think I kiss good?" he asked with a jaunt in his step.

Chapter 18

Esoong waited until the square box of the room was empty before he transformed slowly into a four dimensional hologram. He stretched his neck, trying to get the kink out, wondering how these humans carried around the melon shape so easily.

He flexed his muscles, well, as much muscle as a hologram could have and flex.

The gurgling, bubbling box of water that sat alone on the top of the wooden shelf intrigued him. The colors slowed, reflecting off his own and he felt like it was a spirit from Zorone. He picked at the flashing neon light. Heat seared through him. He thrust it down into the water. He was transitioning from a hologram into an Earthling.

Fury filled him over the object's attempt to bite him. Shoving his hand into the pot of warm water, he grabbed the flickering gold object as it kept darting in and out behind a bubbling treasure chest.

He'd only ever seen something like this once on Planet Zorone. It was food then, a source of energy, and if he was going to put up with the weird time changes, not to mention the global warming on Earth, he was going to need substance until he could locate what he came here for.

It took several tries before he could reach the amphibian. At least that's what they called it on his home planet. He was used to bigger fish, ones that were distinct cousins to that creature in Scotland that humans were too stupid to photograph. All they had to do was film at night. Every alien in their right mind knew that. But then, humans were stupid. That's how come they only ruled one planet.

Swallowing the wet creature whole, he belched. It wasn't nearly as filling as the ones on Zorone. He searched for something more substantial. The furry animal was nowhere to be seen, so he had to do the next best thing. Every Zoroneite knew if you couldn't find food, water was what you needed to survive.

He leaned over the bowl of liquid and drank, the fluid running down his chin and out through his stomach.

Esoong swore. He should have realized in the transition stage that food remained in his stomach, water not so much. He glanced at the floor and saw the puddle. Dragging some of the material tossed on the floor, he used it to sop up the evidence.

When he was satisfied, he peered around for something of substance and ate some flakes that were sitting beside the box. Licking his finger, he ate the rest of the smelly food. It did nothing to quench his appetite.

He didn't know how he was supposed to hold Earth hostage when he couldn't even hold water.

This was more challenging than he'd thought.

Chapter 19

"So we're all set for tomorrow?" I said into the phone as I wandered into my room, set a half-filled glass of water on the night table and plopped onto the bed.

"Yep, my dad is going to drop me off when he comes to pick up your mom. He said I could sleep over if that was okay with your mom," Sawyer said.

"Sounds good." I jumped off the bed and went over to the aquarium to feed Goldie. I couldn't see her but that was nothing new. She liked to hide. The fish food container was empty. I'll have to add it onto mom's shopping list.

"We could ask for anything right now and our parents would go for it," Sawyer said in his typical fashion. "Okay, got to go and grab a bite before bed. How's your sister?"

"What did you say?" I shook the phone and then put the receiver back to my ear. "I think there's something wrong with the reception. I thought you asked about Demi."

"I did. Did she get home from work okay?" he asked, like it was important.

"I guess so. She's in the shower using all the hot water and mine will be freezing cold."

I hung up from Sawyer, wondering if he'd been hit in the head or something.

Jane Greenhill

It didn't take long for my room to get messy again as I noticed a pile of clothes by the fish tank.

I went to pick them up. I know. How odd that I would do something like that! Strange but true, and I was surprised to find them wet. Great! Mom really was losing it when she put my clothes in the room without putting them in the dryer.

Also the water in the tank looked a little low. Probably when she cleaned it, she didn't fill it up as far as normal.

What was I going to do with my mom?

I was going to have to ream her out. She was letting her duties slip because of a boy.

I climbed into bed and promptly fell asleep with my comic books spread open all over my bed. Lucky began to softly whine and scampered up to my pillow. I wasn't sure if it was for my comfort or his.

Chapter 20

Thursday

The teachers piled us with homework, and my back was sore from all the textbooks I had to bring home, and I threw them in the corner of the kitchen. I wasn't in the mood for homework. I was in the mood for a donut or three.

I walked through the kitchen on the way to the television, grabbing donuts from a container on the kitchen table as I went. I flopped down on the leather couch and clicked it on. Dr. Greg was on every channel! How annoying.

"Do I look ok?"

I glanced up to see a woman who had sounded like my mom but looked nothing like the mother I knew. I peered at her hair, which was highlighted and feathered in a way that kept falling into her face. It would probably bug her in the long run, but tonight she looked hot—for a mom.

"Mom, don't you think you should go upstairs and get some more clothes on?" I asked, glancing up at the new red dress that was hardly there. I mean, there were two little straps holding up a piece of material. I think the tea towels in the kitchen were bigger. It was a nice dress, just not for a mom.

My mom.

"Gregory, that's the style." Then my mom twirled around. "Do I seem ok from the back?"

Jeez, what do I look like? A fashion guru?

"Well, at least there's more material there than in the front. Are you sure you have it on the right way?"

"Very funny. Demi, what do you think?" she asked my sister who entered the room, gaping for some reason like a deer caught in the headlights.

"Good, you're chillin', Mom."

I was about to make another comment, but I or maybe Mom was saved by the sound of the doorbell. I jumped off the couch and ran to the door.

"Hey Mr. Finnegan, Sawyer, come on in. My mom's right here." I pulled them into the family room, but Mom had done a disappearing act.

"MOM!"

"There's no need to yell." My mom came through the swinging door from the kitchen. I watched Sawyer's dad check out my mom. His eyes started at the top and went down to her shoes, then back up to her head. Even I could feel the electricity in the room, and it had nothing to do with the light bulbs.

"Sophia, you look gorgeous."

"You clean up pretty well yourself," she giggled.

Oh no, my mom had started that giggling stuff again.

"Okay, well you two kids have a great time and we'll see you when we see you," Sawyer said, pushing them out the door. "Don't you kids do anything I wouldn't do."

"You have my cell phone number if you have any problems, and Demi is coming straight home from work so you two boys shouldn't be alone too long."

"Come on, Sophia! The boys will be fine." Mr. Finnegan put an arm on my mom's back and pushed her gently out the door.

I stood at the window and waved, not that I really wanted to, but I knew Mom would expect me to.

As the headlights of the car shone in the window, I waved again, and then Sawyer yanked me away.

"Ok, let's get this party started." He jumped up on the couch, dancing.

"We're not having a party. My mom would kill me," I said firmly.

"It's just a figure of speech. Jeez!"

****

Hunger pains forced Esoong out of the confines of the book and into the boy's room. As the variety of colors changed into the Komodo dragon shape, his tail was the first appendage to become solid.

He slithered out, shaking off the feeling of remoteness that always accompanied his leaving the nest and protection of the book.

He climbed onto a shelf, then another, until he was level with what his body craved, with what his system needed to survive.

Using his claws to scratch the surface of the plastic container, he freed what he needed, for what he'd come to Earth in search of—quartz.

****

"Ok, I'm leaving now, I won't be late."

"Demi, how are you feeling after last night and all?" Sawyer went over to her and put a hand on her arm, which she shrugged off.

"I'm fine. Thanks for asking, really," she said, clipping her nametag onto her uniform.

"Sis, remember to bring home donuts tonight. Last night she left in a real snit and didn't bring us any treats."

She gazed at us both, and for some reason kept looking at Sawyer longer than me. She left, the sound of her sneakers squeaking down the walkway.

"I think your sister had a bit more on her mind than your stomach," Sawyer said.

I stood stunned. In fact, you could have knocked me over with a feather. Sawyer was defending my flesh and blood. Heck, I wasn't even fond of doing that. Something was going on here and I think I knew what.

"Sawyer Finnegan, you have the hots for my sister. Major grossness." I stared at him.

"Shut up!" He winged a pillow from the couch at me. "I'm just concerned after what happened last night."

"I give. What happened last night?" I asked, surprised he knew an event going on in my family I didn't.

"She was attacked," he said simply. "Don't worry though. I stopped the attack and she's fine." He blew on his fingernails and rubbed them on his shirt.

"You're such a liar. She was not attacked. If she was, she would have said something to me and Mom."

"She didn't want me to call the cops, so she probably didn't want to worry your mom. Besides, your mom looked kind of preoccupied." He smirked.

"My mom is never too busy to worry about us kids. So what happened?"

"I guess she was leaving work and some guy jumped her. I was on my way back from Chy's, my dad wanted some potato chips. I recognized Demi and to bug her I interrupted her. At first I thought she was in the bushes making out with her boyfriend."

"She doesn't have a boyfriend."

"I know that now." Sawyer ignored me and continued. "I scared the guy off and brought her home. End of story." He shrugged nonchalantly.

I followed him into the kitchen which seemed to draw him like a magnet whenever he was in my house. He rooted through the cupboard, found a package of popcorn and after unwrapping it from the plastic, he tossed it in the microwave. After pushing the buttons, he poured himself a soda, then bent over and slurped the foam off the top.

"So what do you want to do? Watch TV? The movie 'Signages'?" I asked, referring to my favorite movie of all time, as I got myself a glass of soda.

"No, I want to see what's so damned important about this stupid comic book."

"What are you talking about?" I asked, surprised he even cared about the book.

"Demi said when that jerk attacked her last night he said for you to bring the comic book to the school yard tonight, if you want to keep your family safe," Sawyer said, just as the microwave dinged, almost as if it was emphasizing the point.

"You're making that up," I said, grabbing a handful of popcorn.

"Well, I guess we'll just have to wait and find out, won't we? Come on, let's go and see the stupid comic book."

"Sawyer, I got a phone call yesterday. I thought it was a crank call, but now I'm not so sure."

"What did they say?" Sawyer asked. I had his

undivided attention. Even the popcorn rated a distant second.

"He said I would get the latest gaming system if I gave him the comic book."

"That sounds ok." Sawyer took a deep breath.

"When I told him to forget it, I was going to keep it, he threatened me. Sawyer, what is so damned important about this comic book? People are getting pretty stressed out and I don't think it's because it's a first edition."

"That's what I intend to find out. Let's go!"

The phone interrupted our mission.

Chapter 21

"I hope the boys are ok," Sophia Adams said as she sunk deeper into the leather passenger seat.

"Why don't you phone them? Then you'll realize they're fine and it will put that pretty little mind of yours at ease," Rex said, slipping an arm across the back of the seat.

"Maybe I'll do that. I'll phone them before your guests arrive and then I'll be able to concentrate on the evening. I'm sorry I'm such a worrier."

"Here, use mine." He reached toward the dash and handed her his cell phone. "Save your battery."

Grinning, she took the phone from him and punched in her numbers.

"You really didn't need to do that, I have you on speed dial," he said.

Feeling slightly smug, she waited through the five rings before it was finally answered.

"Hello!"

"Gregory, it's Mom. I just wanted to make sure everything was ok and you boys weren't having any problems."

"Jezz Mom, you've only been gone less than an hour. Sawyer just made some popcorn and we're heading to my bedroom to look at my comic books."

"Did Demi get off to work?"

"Yep, no prob. Mom, I have to go. Lucky wants in.

Bye, have fun and QUIT WORRYING."

"Bye, sweetheart," she giggled.

"That was my mom checking up on us." I opened the door and let the dog in. Instead of waiting at the treat cupboard much in the same way that Sawyer did when he came over, Lucky ran through the kitchen and straight upstairs.

"What a psycho dog you have. Are you ready to go upstairs and see the dreaded comic book?" Sawyer grabbed the bag of popcorn and soda.

"Sawyer let's get the dang thing over with. Something always gets in the way. I'm really creeped out though about what happened to Demi. I mean, if you hadn't come along when you did, who knows what might have happened." I was a little apprehensive, I must admit. This freebee was controlling my life and I didn't like it. I was still undecided what I should do with the stupid thing.

"Not to worry. Super Sawyer is on the scene. Now let's go."

I entered my room and stopped.

There was an energy circle in the middle, the colors glowing like a lava lamp. I stood still, mesmerized by the thing that was taking control of my space. My bed shifted out of the way, as if it too was afraid.

The light continued to evolve. It made a slight growling sound when I realized it was growing and flourishing.

It took the shape of a Komodo dragon but stood upright. It had an extra arm along its side and a strange furry thing hanging out of its mouth.

Oh Crapola, it had eaten Lucky.

Chapter 22

Sophia got out of the luxury car at the Planet Garden Restaurant and strolled up the concrete steps, feeling like a princess.

The doorman, dressed head to toe in a black tux, held open the door for them, bowing slightly.

She took a deep breath as she took in the humongous baskets suspended from the cathedral ceiling. Bursting and overflowing with tropical flowers in red, yellow as well as the regal Bird of Paradise, the theme carried through to the table runners and napkins.

"This is as beautiful as I imagined it would be," she gushed.

"The owner is a friend of mine," Rex said, then turned to the headwaiter and gave him his name.

"Follow me, please."

"Dolly, Fred, this is Sophia Adams," Rex said, making the introductions.

"Hi, nice to meet you." Fred, an obvious cowboy if the tie, hat and decorated cowboy shirt were any indication, held out his hand.

"Hi, I'm Dolly and I am not the trophy wife." She laughed; a fiery redhead with her chest falling out of her low-cut dress.

"No sireebob, I got it right the first time. Besides, if I ever looked at another woman, present company included, Dolly'd have me castrated before the sun came up. Wouldn't you, girlie?"

"Damn straight!"

Sophia ordered a glass of white wine, while Rex told the waiter he'd like a scotch and soda.

"Hit me again, barkeep? What about you, Dolly Mae? Like another frilly drink?" Without waiting for his wife to answer, he nodded to the waiter.

"So how do you folks know each other?" Fred asked.

"Our sons are friends," Sophia said, barely able to keep a straight face.

"We never had the pleasure of having boys, just our girls, girls that have their daddy wrapped right around their little pinkie. Yep, Flora Mae and Petunia Mae know how to keep their old man right where they want them."

"How old are they?"

"Flora Mae, now let me see. Had her nine months to the day we were married, a honeymoon baby she was, so she's thirty-five and Petunia Mae is thirty-three."

"Those are unusual names. I named my kids after names I found in a baby book," Sophia admitted.

"Well, we figured that our chillens would get famous all on their lonesome," Dolly Mae said, gulping down the liquid in her glass.

"Wow, you must have been a child bride, you look so young to have kids that old," Sophia said.

"Actually, I was. My daddy had a shotgun waiting for Fred when he came to visit. Said he was marrying me or else."

"I was afraid to find out what the 'or else' was." He winked, three times in repetition.

Sophia opened up her menu and studied it, trying to keep from laughing.

"Sophia, they're playing our song," Rex said. "Tell Fred what you'd like to order and he can tell the waiter while we're dancing."

"I'll have the Tiger Shrimp," she said.

"Grrr," Fred yelled across the table.

"Are you having a good time?" Rex asked, as he held Sophia in his arms. She admitted to herself she liked the feel of her skin against his, even if his neck skin seemed a little rough. Together they swayed to the band's rendition of the Top 40 current hits.

"I am. Thank you for inviting me. Your clients are really fun people. I didn't realize we had a song," she said.

He laughed. "I thought you needed rescuing. They are salt of the Earth types. A little rednecky for some people's tastes, but I do a lot of business with him and he's never screwed me over."

Sophia lost herself in the familiar vibrations of the song.

"Sophia, I've wanted to ask you out for a long time, but I didn't think you were quite ready. You always seemed kind of distant whenever I dropped Sawyer off."

"I'm sorry if I gave that impression," she said as the music stopped.

"Nothing to be sorry for, you've been worth the wait." He leaned forward and kissed her gently on the lips.

The move made her nervous. She wasn't sure if she was ready for his step. Cripes, it had been so many years since someone got to first base that she couldn't remember the stages. Holy cow, first base. Heck, she hadn't even gotten anyone to want to go to bat on her team!

She said the first thing that came to her. "I wonder how the boys are?"

"Sophia, the boys are fine. They can look after themselves. I've been leaving Sawyer alone for over a year now and never had any problems."

"Well, there are probably stories you've never heard about."

"Very true." He laughed. "How about I have you until ten and then you call the boys? Is that a deal?"

"What are we going to do until ten? The band looks like they're taking a break." She nodded towards them as the four band members put their instruments down and headed off the stage.

"I'm sure I can think of a thing or two. Would you like to stay inside with the clients or take a walk outside under the stars?"

"Definitely the stars."

"A girl after my own heart. Let's go and sneak out through these doors here. Then they won't see us and we won't be dragged into conversations we'd rather not have."

"What about dinner?"

"Ok, first the shrimp, then the stars. Deal?"

"Deal!"

****

The strange creature changed in front of my eyes. I almost peed my pants. This was like a weird episode of some television show. But what made this so scary was this was real life. It looked like a mutant Komodo dragon. I'd learnt a bit about them in one of those weekly tabloids. Mom had the magazine lying on the coffee table and the front page had a picture of that hot chick Alabama West whose husband got his toe nipped at by the dragon at the zoo, so I read up on them.

In fact, I'd even done my class speech on the subject.

I wiped my sweaty palms on my shorts when I remembered my opening sentence. A Komodo dragon could eat a ninety-pound pig in less than twenty minutes. The equivalent would be a person eating three hundred and twenty quarter pound hamburgers.

Shit! Where was my dog?

"Gregory!" Sawyer whispered my name.

I felt drawn towards the force field, like a magnet was pulling me closer and closer.

I forgot Sawyer was behind me. I felt him grasp my shoulder and yank me backwards. I was mesmerized by the colors, by the twirling motion of the mist. One minute it seemed to be a well-defined dragon, the next it changed into a swirling array.

"What should we do? I think that's part of Lucky," Sawyer whispered.

His words knocked sense into me and I grabbed at my dog's tail and pulled with all my might. Sawyer wrapped his arms around my waist to give me the extra leverage.

A snarling, yelping sound encircled the room and as I have one last mighty tug, Lucky flew out of the creature's mouth and after licking me across the face, ran out of the room and downstairs when in the sudden silence of the room, I could hear her lapping water.

I wish I was older. I was going to need a stronger drink than that if this continued.

"Now what?"

Some supernatural force was helping me because I knew what to do. I saw the movie 'Signages' and knew that aliens didn't like water. So I grabbed my glass of water from the night table and threw it, glass and all.

A loud piercing moan escaped through the room and the creature once filled with bright neonish colors now was fading to dullness, the colors eventually turning to a yucky green and a pukey yellow.

It half flew, half floated across the room and as soon as it was over the comic book, I jumped up and closed the cover, sitting on it so that whatever it was wouldn't escape.

I peered over at Sawyer, who must have gotten in the way of some of the water, because his face was covered in beads.

"Well, that was sure something." He grinned.

"I think we'd better get this comic book to the school yard. That gaming system is starting to look pretty good right now. I want to get that frickin thing out of my house."

"Gregory, your mother would wash your mouth out with soap, if she could hear the language coming out of it."

"My mom would understand. Let's go." I grabbed the comic book and the bag of freebees I had gotten from Max Bombard. I didn't want anything from him in my house ever again. I would be redecorating my room in the near future. Jasmine Alberta would be front and center.

Chapter 23

"Rex, I just tried the boys and there was no answer." Sophia came back to the table wringing her hands.

"Little lady, botox will take care of those forehead lines," Dolly Mae said.

"So would not having kids." Sophia leaned towards Rex and wiped a light dust off his sleeve she hadn't noticed before.

"Did you want to go?" he asked, only mildly concerned of the fate of his son.

"Rex, have you been playing on the road? You're covered with rock dust!" Fred asked, wrapping an arm around Dolly Mae.

"Ummm, no. So what do you want to do about the boys?" Rex asked, ignoring his client.

"You know what? Knowing them, they have the music cranked and couldn't hear the phone. I'll try again in a bit. I'm sure they're fine and besides, I'm having too good a time for this to end," she said determinedly.

"That's my girl," Rex said, topping off her wine glass. "How about another moonlight stroll?"

She grinned and pushed away from the table. "Well, if you insist." She was determined to put being a mother on hold for the night, if it was at all possible.

****

"Ok, dweeb one and dweeb two, where are you?" Demi yelled through the house as she entered the back door. She dropped a full box of donuts on the barn-board kitchen table.

She kicked off her running shoes and undid her polyester shirt leaving it open, revealing the white t-shirt underneath.

"Hi, Lucky. Where is Gregory?"

She headed upstairs. After stopping in her own room to fully remove her work shirt and throw on a Billy Tenent sweatshirt, she checked out her brother's room.

"Shit," she said to the four walls. "Lucky, where did they go?" If they were screwing with her when she was supposed to be baby-sitting them, Gregory would be doing chores until he was an old man.

She re-entered her brother's room, something she usually avoided at all possible costs, and bent down, investigating the broken glass shards and wet carpet. His container of rocks empty on the floor.

She wasn't overly familiar with his room, but when she gazed at the bookshelf over the computer she noticed something missing.

The gold binder, his pride and joy.

A chill travelled through her and despite the sweatshirt, she shivered.

"Oh no, they went to the school yard." She turned and flew out of the room, bounded down the stairs, Lucky nipping at her heels. "Lucky, stay!" She ran into the kitchen, scrunched on her shoes without bothering to tie them and ran from the house. "Ok, come on, Lucky, let's go save them."

Minutes later, she ran back through the house,

looking for a weapon, any kind. If the jerk who attacked her was there, she was going to hit him good. She owed him a fright like the one he'd given her. Spotting what she'd need, she scooped it up and rushed from the house, towards the schoolyard a block away, praying she wasn't too late to save her stupid brother and his friend.

****

"So, what do you think that was all about? I mean, what happened in your room?" Sawyer asked, scared, but trying to keep up to me.

Whenever Sawyer was nervous or frightened, he'd bite his lip, a trait he'd been concealing since Grade Three when he was caught throwing wet paper towels in the boy's bathroom at school. Today, I noticed he'd bitten through the outer skin and blood was dripping down his lip like he'd had a vampire's feast.

I was a man on a mission. I had to get rid of this devilish comic book. It was one thing for the people who wanted the evil thing back to attack my sister, but they'd really ticked me off when the creature tried to eat my dog.

I was pissed.

We got to Hugh Jackman Public School and I didn't know what to expect, but not this. There was no one there. I stared up into the stars, searching.

"Ok, where's the spaceship?" Sawyer asked, echoing my thoughts.

"I think we're the only ones here," I said, marching over to the gazebo that bordered the pavement between the school and the portables.

I went inside the wooden structure and flopped down on the bench beside the plaque that read it had been erected in nineteen seventy-five. Crikey, this building was a landmark.

I dropped the bags at my feet and put my head in my hands.

"Sawyer, what do you think that creature was?"

"Didn't it seem familiar to you? You are after all the comic book guru!"

"Come on, what are you talking about?" I asked, confused. I bent down and plucked a stray dandelion, picking it apart. The smell of it invaded my nose and the weed played havoc with my allergies. I sneezed three times in repetition.

"The monster that came to life in your bedroom was from the latest story by Max Bombard. You had a real live Zoroneite in your house," Sawyer said, "I'm shocked that you didn't come to the same conclusion."

I threw the dandelion against the wall of the gazebo. "Crapola! I never noticed. I was more concerned about getting Lucky out of that thing's mouth than I was about anything else. You're right. How do we get rid of it?"

I shivered, more from the cold air that was signifying the approach of fall than from his words, though they weren't helping matters any. I should have brought a sweatshirt.

"Maybe they planned it. Maybe they didn't want you to finish it. Something always happened so we couldn't finish it. Maybe that's how they keep control of your mind. Doodoodoodoo." Sawyer made the sound of the annoying music they always play in horror movies just before the star opens the door heading down to the basement and is mutilated by whatever monster lay behind it.

"Shut up! Nothing is controlling my mind." I kicked at the wooden floor of the gazebo and unintentionally kicked the bag.

That was a mistake.

Like a colorful puff of smoke, a blurry rainbow swirled from within.

Chapter 24

As the comic book slid out of the bag, something tapped me on my left shoulder. I jumped, nearly crying out.

I turned in full karate stance to see Demi standing there. From the look on her face, I was in bigger trouble from her than from whatever Zoroneite might be in the bag. "Sorry, I didn't mean to startle you but what are you two doing out here? You should be glad I got home before Mom or she'd wring your neck. What the heck are you doing here?" Demi repeated

"You should know, Miss I Got Attacked and Didn't Tell Anyone," I said rudely.

Her mouth gaped open in surprise. She glanced over at Sawyer, then back to me.

I couldn't help myself. I was the man of the family and it really bugged me that Sawyer came to my sister's rescue.

"It was nothing. Sawyer, I asked you not to say anything." Her tone was pissed.

Sawyer shrugged. "No, to correct you, you told me not to call the police. You didn't say anything about telling Gregory. I'm sorry, I thought he should know."

"Whatever," she said, sounding tired. "It's all water under the bridge. Nothing happened, so let's just drop it."

"Fraid that's not going to happen, girlie," a voice

sounding like a distorted voice box bellowed.

This time all three of us jumped as a man came out from behind the nearest school portable. Immediately I backed up, protecting Demi. Sawyer stood beside me and together we created a human shield.

As he came closer to us, away from the shadow of the building, he removed his sunglasses.

It was the guy who'd given us all the free stuff at ComTol, the one who kept whispering in Max Bombard's ear as he stood behind the chair.

"Who are you and what do you want?" I asked with more bravado than I felt.

"Jonathon Crawley at your service. And I think you're smart enough to know what I want."

"You're welcome to it," I said, picking up the bag with the comic in it and tossing it towards him.

"Well you gave that up pretty easy. I thought I'd have to get forceful with you. I guess Max was right. You're just a stupid punk after all." He grabbed the bag and pulled out the book.

All of a sudden, it flew out of his hands and hit the pavement. A wind of almost hurricane proportions blew across the playground; the swings began to move and squeaked on their chains. Tumbleweed rolled across the yellowed grass, the sky turned black, green, then yellow.

With the speed of the Tasmanian devil, the comic book's secret spun into life. The creature that had developed in my room was now tenfold. It was half as large as the gazebo and as we stared at it, it did the strangest thing.

The fully evolved Komodo dragon with an extra arm stood upright and stomped over to the kid's play area. Ignoring the swings and slides, it crouched down on all four legs and began to munch the stones that lined the playground. It would pick out certain ones and eat them, throwing away the ones it didn't appear to care for.

"He's picking out the quartz," Mr. Crawley told us in a thoughtful voice. "Their species need the microcrystalline to survive. That's why he had to come to Earth, to save his planet."

There was a pile reaching to the top of the portable filled with discarded rocks. A burp of enormous proportions filled the air and a fart that would make any boy proud had been released. It was all Sawyer and I could do not to high five.

"Ewww," Demi said, waving the air in front of her.

Resting on its tail, it lay on its back, scratched its belly, and then as the four of us with our mouths gaping watched, it changed shape into a more solid being.

Seeming as it was filled up, at least from the size of its bloated stomach, its strong claws began to pick at its scaly skin and its long, forked tongue began to lick outside its mouth.

The pole lights in the playground flickered on and off almost in the method of a disco ball as they crackled and sparked.

The moon that had been helping to brighten the field now became shrouded in clouds, leaving us in darkness.

Slowly, the clouds shifted and the ground began to glow. I looked over at Demi and she grabbed the other bag that was lying in the gazebo. I think she was planning on a quick getaway.

I know I was.

As the moon became our main source of light, I stood in shock as Max Bombard materialized in front of me.

Castings from the creature's skin now surrounded the prone body of the comic book creator, reminding me of a snake shedding its skin.

Jonathon Crawley rushed to his boss's side and grabbed onto his hand, helping him to his feet. He stood, somewhat shakily, almost as if he wasn't used to standing without a tail to balance him.

I moved closer to my sister and took the bag from her hand. I didn't want her involved in this mess any more than she needed to be. I wanted her to be able to run fast to get away.

"Sawyer," I whispered. "Go! Take Demi and go. I can handle these two. I want you to phone Mom. Tell her what happened!"

"I'm not leaving you here by yourself. This is nuts. Who ever heard of a Komodo dragon turning into a person? This is a frigging nightmare." Demi glanced over at us.

"More like Dr. Jekyll and Mr. Hyde," Sawyer commented.

"Shut up! All of you! I have super sensitive hearing," Max Bombard yelled.

"Sir, calm down," Crawley said. "You'll upset yourself."

"You are the one who created this mess. What the heck were you thinking giving away the comic book? If you'd used that melon you call a brain, none of this would have happened. I've lived the secret double life since I got back from Russia. No one had to find out. No one had to know. Now we're going to have to silence these kids, each and every one of them."

"No, you don't. We know how to keep a secret. We promise we won't tell a soul. We promise," Demi said, close to tears. "Please, he's my little brother and I was supposed to look after him. He and his friend snuck out of the house to return your belongings to you. Now you have everything. We'll just go home and forget this ever happened. Come on, Gregory, Sawyer, let's go."

"Not so fast!" Max Bombard said in a tone that didn't invite arguments. "If I can morph out of that stupid comic book to become a human/dragon, I think I deserve some respect."

"What?" My sister turned around, impatiently. "You got what you wanted. We promised to keep quiet. What more do you need?"

"I've eaten all the quartz here. I need more."

"With the size of your stomach, I think you should maybe try vegetarian. Rocks can't be that good for the digestive system. Look at how bloated you are."

"Demi, watch it," I warned.

"Listen to your annoying brother, Demi. Watch it! I don't appreciate guff from a female punk like you. Now where can I get more quartz?" Max Bombard demanded.

"Sir, let them go. We can just hit the playgrounds in the area. That should fill you up enough and then we'll find a gravel pit for you to take home."

"That won't work. In order to control Earth, I need to control their resources. Quartz is an abundant and untapped mineral. If the stupid Earthlings would get their heads out of their butts long enough to do some research, they'd see the possibilities." Max Bombard fumed.

"I don't know what planet you came from, oh right Zorone, but we already know that. We've utilized its properties in a lot of high-tech devices. It's only a matter of time before our mineral base provides most of our basic power supplies," I said with certainty.

Max narrowed his beady eyes at me. "You think you're so smart. If that's true, then why are you Earth people still killing your planet? I'll tell you why. Instant gratification. You might have some knowledge of this mineral now but not enough. We're already light years ahead of you. Maybe if you didn't spend so much bloody money working on a Space Port when everything you need to survive for the next billion years is staring you right in the face."

"So when you steal the quartz what are you going to do?" Sawyer asked, quiet until now.

"I have to ensure that there's enough for my fellow Zoroneites, and then they'll travel here much the same way I have, in the host body of the humans that spend all the money to travel to space." His eyes swept over us triumphantly. "That's right. In a few short months, this will be known as Zorone II, and you will be our slaves, working for us, mining the quartz," Max Bombard said, his voice taking on the tone and speech pattern of an evil scientist.

Which I guess he was.

How had my love of comic books turned into a fight to save Earth?

Chapter 25

"Rex, I'm starting to get worried. I tried home again and there wasn't an answer," Sophia said, wringing her hands together. She rolled the dinner fork over a few times, trying to calm herself down. The shrimp she'd eaten at dinner swam in her stomach, as if still alive.

Rex put his arm around her shoulder and rubbed lightly. "I'm sure it's nothing, Sophia. They do have a holiday tomorrow from school, with that teacher development day. They're probably having so much fun, watching horror movies turned up so high, they'll need hearing aids by the time they're our age." He kissed the top of her head. "Doesn't Demi have a phone?"

"She had it shut off when she's at work, but I'll try her again, just on the off chance." Glancing down at her slim gold watch, she marked how late it was.

"What time does she get off?" Rex asked, draping his arm across the back of her chair.

"Usually it's midnight, but sometimes if it's quiet, she gets to leave early." Sophia punched in the digits. Her fingers curled around the cell phone, tighter with each ring.

"Hello!" Demi's voice floated through her receiver.

"Thank Goodness! Hi honey, it's Mom. Is everything ok?"

"Umm, yep, Mom, we're fine. Gregory and I are getting along fine. Sawyer isn't even so bad. We're playing nice just like we do in school."

****

"Hang up that phone," Max Bombard hissed.

Demi snapped the cell phone closed.

"Calm down, I couldn't hang up on my mom. She would know something was up." She flipped her hair over her shoulder and gave the Max-creature a 'duh' stare. "Plus I'd get in big trouble when I got home."

"That's if we make it home," Sawyer murmured.

"My thoughts exactly," Max Bombard snarled again.

"So what's it like on Planet Zorone?" I asked, stalling. I don't know what for, but any kind of talk that kept us alive and the planet out of the claws of evil was favorable.

"Just like the comic books, punk. Where do you think I got my inspiration? It's not like Max Bombard has any imagination. That's why it was so easy to hop on board the Russian spacecraft while he was there."

"Aren't you one and the same?"

"Bully no! Brabora, the leader of my planet had it all worked out. When the Russian spacecraft came within range, we staged a meteorite shower," he boasted. "It actually hit their rocket, causing their controls to go out of whack for a short period allowing enough time for me to get on board and into the space suit of the weakest link. Then it was nothing to get to Earth and end up in the middle of a comic book. Quite simple really." Max Bombard or whoever he was yawned, almost like he was bored with the whole event.

Yeah, I guess I'd be bored too, after a tryst like

that.

"I have to go to the bathroom," I admitted, crossing my legs trying to hold it in.

"Well, I guess you're just going to have to go in your pants. There's not a washroom here," Crawley said.

"Come on, I can't pee in my pants. My sister would never let me hear the end of it. Can I just go around the side of the portable?"

"Fine, but stay where we can see you."

"I'm hungry," Demi said, appearing to catch onto my idea, distracting them while I grabbed the plastic bag and headed towards the portable to have my pee.

"Want a rock?" the creature asked.

"No, I don't want a rock. I have a chocolate bar in my purse." A gleam only a brother would recognize entered her eyes. "Mind if I get it?"

Without waiting for an answer, I watched her reach into her purse, and instead of pulling out the chocolate bar, she had in her hand a can of whipped cream.

Flipping the cap off, she aimed the nozzle straight at Max Bombard and fired. The gooey whipped topping covered his face like a poor man's Santa Claus.

"What the heck are you doing? You're going to blind me," he screeched, his hands clawing at his face, trying to remove the foamy substance.

"If she doesn't, I will." I grabbed the plastic bag, pulled out the ray gun that had been a freebee at the ComTol and fired it. I had filled it with my bodily fluids. His eyes bugged out and he screamed like a banshee. I had no idea what a banshee was, but I heard it once on television and it was loud. Just like Max was now.

"Are you trying to kill me? My species isn't used to toxic waste."

"That's not toxic, it's my pee," I said. "You know what? You're a real jerk. I'm never buying another one of your comic books again as long as I live and that's going to be a heck of a lot longer than you." I cocked the gun again and hit him with another blast of liquid. "Not only that, your website is so shut down." In a blur he slowly melted into a puff of smoke.

But I wasn't done yet.

I was afraid he'd come back.

Not as Max Bombard, but as the Komodo dragon.

Komodo dragons on Earth have no natural enemies, but in reading the Warrior series I knew that the Komodo dragons in the series did.

Saying a silent prayer to whoever might be listening, I waited until the moon broke free from the clouds once again.

Grabbing my sister's purse, I dumped the contents onto the ground.

"What the heck do you think you're doing? You are so cleaning that up," Demi yelled.

Great! Here I was intent on saving Earth and my sister was ragging on me.

I heard a car door slam shut and out of the corner of my eye, I saw two adults approaching us.

"Gregory, what is going on here? You are in so much trouble. I told you not to go out but as soon as my back is turned, you trot off with Sawyer," my mom yelled across the parking lot. "And you, young lady, what are you doing here as well? You're supposed to be watching them. You are all so grounded."

"Mom, keep back." I frantically waved at her. I

didn't want her to have to see what I was about to do.

"Dad, he's right. You guys need to stay away from this. It'll just suck you in like it did us," Sawyer called out, his arm now wrapped around Demi.

I did a double take at their attachment. I could handle only one surreal event at a time. Them I would deal with later.

The spinning, whirling illusion morphed into a bigger, stronger dragon and I knew from reading the comic books to stay away from the third arm or whatever the heck it was. It only had one purpose and that was to maim, or worse, kill any attackers.

As the moon escaped from the cloud covering, I opened my sister's eye shadow. I tilted and angled the mirror so that it reflected the rays of the moon and held my breath.

Komodo dragons from the evil planet Zorone don't like the moon's rays, especially when it was the second full moon in a calendar month. Or as my mom liked to call it—the Blue Moon.

I held on to the mirror with all my force, the dragon trying to use whatever superpowers it might have to jerk it away from me. I planted my feet in the soil of the playground, since most of the rocks were gone. I felt the tug, but I was stronger than the forces of evil on Planet Zorone.

A southeasterly wind picked up, scattering the chip bags and pop cans across the grass, but still I held on. I had a vision of a wizard and what I wouldn't give for a magical wand right here and now. But unfortunately, this wasn't a story, it wasn't make-believe. It was real. Too real.

I scrutinized the creature in front of me; weakened,

he fell backwards, his tail no longer strong enough to support the weight. Desperately he clawed at the air, trying to right himself.

"Crapola!" I said aloud, and Mom didn't even correct me.

I turned to see Mom and Rex gasping at the alien, mouths open. I was going to be in big trouble if I lived to tell her about it.

I observed the Blue Moon losing its strength; a cloud mass was passing over and the alien wasn't dead. It struggled and began to exhibit signs of life again. Slowly it reared its ugly head, and I was helpless.

I was in its path, too drained from the mirror ordeal to move.

"My name is Esoong," the creature sneered in a slow-speaking and mechanical voice. It lifted its head, seeming to get strength back into his neck.

Suddenly, my face was wet. Lucky licked me, then Lucky climbed across my stomach and began barking and snapping at the alien.

My dog renewed my strength and I scrambled back on my heels, watching the moon, but it was still dark. The clouds weren't shifting as fast as I would have liked.

Esoong became empowered and Lucky had a fight on her paws. Dragon against dog, and I was afraid who was going to win. There was a reason that Komodo dragons had no natural enemies on earth; they were fearless. My dog, on the other paw, crawled under the bed if there was a crack of thunder within five miles.

Demi broke free of Sawyer. "Esteroing, or whatever your stupid name is. Leave my dog alone." She kicked at it with her sneakers, not having much effect but getting an A for effort in my book.

I struggled onto all fours and glanced up to see my mom now in the fracas.

"You &^%$^% alien. You think we're (*&&^^& Earthlings, but we've been here long before you and we'll be here long after you; you're just an exhibit in the museum." Mom used words that would make a sailor blush.

She held one of her fancy dress shoes in her hand, and began to throttle Esoong. He snapped and clawed at her, but Lucky and Demi together were no match.

"Our &^%^& planet is not for sale and you can just leave my family out of this." She emphasized the last sentence with heavier thrusts of her shoe. I don't think that's really what they were meant for, but I saw the glow of the gold braid and it hung down, obviously broken.

Wait a minute. Glow of the gold braid. Yes, the clouds had moved.

I scratched through the grass and found the mirror. I positioned it correctly at the moon and Lucky barked loudly when Esoong puddled into the ground, a small faint swirling of colors.

I dumped out Demi's retainer and used some nearby sticks to pick up the Zoroneite. I scooped it into the plastic container along with three stones that weren't consumed.

"Will it be back?" Demi asked, bending and gathering her belongings, not saying a word about her retainer.

"Nope. That's why I put those rocks in with it. You noticed that when he was eating he picked out the quartz and left the other ones." I got a chorus of nods before continuing. "The other ones, the brown ones, are fatal to their systems."

"What? That's crazy," Sawyer said, bending down to help Demi.

"No, he's correct." We looked as one towards Jonathon Crawley who had been silent up until now.

"Thanks for all your help, man," I said, somewhat perturbed.

"Hey, I helped as much as that guy did." He pointed to Sawyer's dad.

"That's true, Dad. Why didn't you help? Boy, even Gregory's mom got in and beat the guy with her shoe."

"My new two-hundred-dollar shoes."

"You paid two hundred dollars for shoes? That is just so typically hypocritical. Jeez, the other day I asked for money for a backpack from my fav store and do I get it? No!" Demi fumed. "But I did get a lecture on the evils of spending hard earned money on junk. Well look who's wasting their money now." She folded her arms and plopped herself down on the bench seat of the gazebo.

"Dad, why didn't you help?" Sawyer asked, sounding disappointed to my ears.

"Your dad is tied up so to speak and has been since the comic book convention." Rex, or who we thought was Rex, spoke and in front of our eyes changed into a six-foot tall Komodo dragon.

Oh no, not another one.

"My name is Brabora and I am the supreme leader of Planet Zorone. I could not trust Esoong to do this alone. It was too important. I gave Esoong a piece of cardboard before he left. I became part of the cardboard, and inserted myself in the comic book, in the cardboard mailer. Alien magic!! I am here to take over Earth and I am…"

"Dead meat!" Crawley raised a smaller version of the gun I had that had been hidden under his jacket and fired twice, once hitting the alien in the extra leg and the second time right between the eyes.

"Where the heck was that gun the first time?" My mom asked, swearing once again. "I was kissed by an alien! EWWW. Where the heck is the real Rex?"

I was going to have to start a swear jar when I got home, and at this rate I'd have a Corvette by summer.

Crawley shrugged. "I wasn't sure what the results would be using it. Hey, I told your son not to use it. I didn't think…"

"That's right, you didn't think. My kids were in danger from some unknown creature from the black lagoon. Yes, I know, Gregory, it was the Planet Zorone." She fluttered her hands in frustration. "And you just stood there like you were having a stroll in the park."

I think the reality of the events finally started to sink in to Mom, because she started to throttle him with her broken shoe. Then for extra emphasis, she took off the other one and hit him some more.

I watched Demi whisper to Sawyer and rub her hand along his face. Man, what is it with those two? They were major grossing me out.

"Mom, stop it! We have more important things to do now, like find Sawyer's dad."

My mom regained her mom composure. "Right, any ideas where your REAL dad might be Sawyer?"

"No, after he dropped you guys off from the convention, he said he was going over to Jackman's

Church to look at some repairs they needed done."

I jumped up and ran towards the old white wooden structure at the back of the school property. The door was never locked and there was a brass collection mailbox at the front for donations. It worked on the honor system, which according to the lack of sounds when I rattled it, there either weren't too many tourists or honest people in town.

I yanked open the barn board door, almost identical to the makeshift computer desk in my room, and yelled for Rex. Mom didn't even correct me and say I should use Mr.

Sawyer, Demi, Mom and Lucky were on my heels.

"Shh, everyone be quiet. Rex, can you hear us?"

Mumbled sounds came from the front of the church. I marched towards the altar but there was nowhere someone could hide.

I ran between the pews, pulling up the seats. When I got to the very last one, it opened and there was Mr. Finnegan, tied up in a makeshift coffin-sized box.

Between Sawyer and me, we helped to lift him out and Mom carefully took the rag out of his mouth. He was in good spirits despite being there for a few days.

"Dad, are you ok?" Sawyer asked.

"Wow, those Planet Zorone time trances are hard on the system," he said, shaking his hands apparently to get the circulation back into his joints. "I feel like I'm just recovering from the flu."

With an arm around each of us, we stumbled out of the church.

"Sawyer, I'm so glad you're ok. Gregory, what gave you the idea to look in here?" he asked, accepting the water bottle from Demi and a half-eaten chocolate bar.

"Let's just say that I was glad I listened that day in class about the Underground Railroad."

Sawyer awkwardly hugged his dad, then went right back to Demi's side and slipped an arm around her waist. I raised my brow like Mom sometimes does to me, but it didn't have any effect.

Mom walked out beside Mr. Finnegan, holding hands. "Umm, Rex, the alien took me to dinner tonight where I met Fred and Dolly Mae."

"They're really a pair, aren't they?" He narrowed his eyes. "I hope he behaved himself."

"Yes, he did. I'm just relieved that they weren't aliens too."

"Well, honey, I always did think they were from another planet." He laughed.

We rounded the corner of the portable to find Mr. Crawley cleaning up the mess and trying to shovel the remaining stones back into position.

"Looks like you're going to be out of a job with your boss gone and all," I said, stroking Lucky's fur.

He shrugged. "I was always the power behind the throne. Maybe I'll try it on my own."

"Over my dead body." Max Bombard in human-form staggered from inside the gazebo. "Wow, that was quite the dream I had."

"It wasn't a dream, it was real life," Crawley told him.

"I'm confused. How could you be in the comic book and in public?" Demi asked.

"When the Esoong took over my body, we time shifted." He looked at me. "When I was in your room, I was Esoong, when I was out in public, I was Max."

"Never mind. Come on, Gregory, I'm sure you have homework to do and a room to clean," Mom said, ignoring the men.

Great! I rescued the world from alien forces but I still had to do spelling. Life was so unfair.

I admit through, I was feeling pretty darn good. I saved the world and didn't think the night could get any better.

I was wrong.

We passed Mindy on the street and she gave me a shy smile, a wave and said she'd see me the next day at school.

After we got home, I immediately headed upstairs and ripped down all my Warrior posters, throwing them into the recycling bin.

Shutting the back door firmly, I headed to the fridge for a well-deserved soda as the phone rang. Wearily I picked up the phone, thinking maybe after tonight I might talk Mom into an updated model with unlimited minutes. There had to be some reward for saving the planet.

"Is this Gregory Mick Adams? This is Jasmine Alberta, and I just got a call from Jonathan Crawley who thinks we should make a movie on the events you went through tonight. I was wondering if we could meet and talk it over."

"You know Jonathan Crawley?" I asked Jasmine. I was talking to Jasmine Alberta? Ok, I admit it was good to save the planet, but imagine talking to Jasmine Alberta and she called you.

"Heck yeah, he's my cousin. If you're good, I'll have Jonathan arrange for us to meet up."

"Yeah, sure." Hey, I can play as cool as the next

guy. Go me!!

I hung up the phone as Lucky trotted into the kitchen, a small disc in her mouth, and dropped it at my feet.

"What have you got girl?" I asked, looking at the title and immediately heading to the sink. I flipped on the trash compactor and listened to the grinding sounds.

"Gregory, what on earth are you doing?" Mom yelled over the noise.

"Mom, it was the game I got at the convention, and Jasmine Alberta just called me."

"Lucky is going to get an extra piece of pizza," Mom said, taking the pizza out of the oven as we all sat around the table, exhausted. "And good, is Jasmine a nice girl from school?"

I was too tired to explain, it would have to wait until tomorrow. Besides, I wanted to keep my conversation with her private a little longer.

"Boys I heard there's a comic book convention in Windsor on Saturday. Want to make a weekend of it?" Mr. Finnegan asked, winking at my mom.

"NOOOOOOOOOOOOOOOOOO!!!!!!!!!!!!!!!!!!!!!!!!!!!!!!"

A word about the author...

Born with a passion to read and write and heavily influenced by Nancy Drew mysteries, Jane Greenhill recalls her first writing experience on an old Underwood typewriter, plunking away at the keys while she wrote about hiding clues in oak trees.

Fast forward through marriage and motherhood, and Jane's now advanced to a laptop and her characters speak to her from other planets.